Liam

Sam's Top Secret Journal:

BOOK 3- MEMORIAL DAY

MR. SEAN ADELMAN
AND
MS. SIRI BARDARSON

ISBN: 1500456829
ISBN 13: 9781500456825

From Sam's Top Secret Journal:

I finished it, my poem for the school assembly tomorrow! Here it is:

Remembering

Remember your family.

Remember your friends.

Remember your dream
that you hold.

Sometimes it's hard to lose
Someone you care about.

Remember the memories of happiness.

Remember the times when they were alive.

The freedom they bring,
the peace for our country.

Thank you for your service.

Abby and Sonja have helped me figure out
what to wear and my friend Andrew will be
sitting next to me at the assembly 'cause
he's giving a short speech about Memorial
Day. I think I will always have a crush on
him even though we are just friends. I like
knowing he will be there! Best friends are the
BEST! Okay, tomorrow... MY BIG DAY!

CHAPTER 1

Moments of Glory

Sam stepped across her younger brother into the back seat of the family van.

"Hey, watch it!" John said and scooted himself as far from his sister as he could.

"Where's Mom?" she asked. John pointed out the front window and Sam craned her neck to see Mom standing in the road and talking to another driver in the student pick-up lane. "Who's she talking to?"

"Andrew's mom," John said. He fidgeted and kicked the seat in front of him. "Let's go! It's vacation!"

Sam sighed and flopped back in her seat. Their family had big plans for the Memorial Day weekend and she shared John's impatience!

Sam sensed the Friday energy in the air as she looked out at the other high school students. They milled around on the sidewalk, chatting and laughing in groups before they went their separate ways for the walk or bus ride home.

An hour ago, all these students had been at the Memorial Day assembly where Sam read her poem.

They looked familiar to her now in their hoodies and jeans with ripped knees but one hour ago, when the principal had introduced Sam and she had walked across the gym floor, the crowded bleachers looked like a wall of strangers. For a split second, Sam froze. She knew she stood out in a crowd, that her Down syndrome made her a bit different and at that moment in the gym she felt the challenge. She was going to stand in front of everyone and do something important!

But she was prepared; Abby and Sonja had practiced with her. They had reminded her to speak slowly so her words wouldn't come out funny and to not hurry when she walked across the gym. Plus, she had on her favorite boots and jeans and T-shirt with the glitter heart on the front. Sam felt strong and beautiful. Yes, she could say that she had felt beautiful.

And then it happened. Someone had booed.

Sitting in the van, the sound echoed in her memory. Sam knew everyone had heard it because of the silence that followed. It was as if the whole assembly was stunned by the meanness of it. Ms. McMasters, the principal, had quickly moved to the podium and looked sternly around the gym while Mr. Rogers, the history teacher, climbed up the bleachers and signaled to a student to follow him and Ms. McMasters out of the assembly.

Everyone watched as Kacey Farmer left the gym, her head held high as though she didn't care. Kacey! No one was surprised because Kacey was trouble with a capital "T". It followed her like a black cloud and rained disaster wherever she went. She had just been expelled from school for getting a tattoo of a fish on her arm. She was admitted back to school on the condition she wear long sleeves.

"Sam!" A voice called from the sidewalk through the open van door. Sam looked out to see Janey Evans, the most popular girl at Seacrest High School, stepping up to the van. "Thanks for the poem, Sam. My big brother is in the Navy."

"You're welcome," Sam smiled.

"Cool boots, too." And with that Janey disappeared into the crowd of students.

"Who's that?" John asked slamming the van door.

"Janey Evans," Sam said softly.

"So how was your moment of glory?" he asked.

"It was good."

When Sam had finished reading the poem, she'd looked up at the crowd and the wall of faces had burst into a wall of sound, students clapped and stomped on the bleacher seats and then stood up and continued clapping until Sam had sat down.

"I got a standing ovation," she said.

"No way!" John said.

Mom opened the door and slid into the driver's seat.

"No way, what?" Mom asked.

Sam stuck her head around the driver's seat and grinned at Mom. She pushed her glasses up on the bridge of her button nose and her hazel eyes sparkled.

"I got a standing ovation!"

Mom caught Sam's eyes in the rearview mirror, "I hope you are proud of yourself. Super brave being in the spotlight like that. What an accomplishment!" She flipped on the ignition and pulled the van out of the crowded parking lot.

"Thanks," Sam beamed.

Mom was right, the assembly had been a big accomplishment and at this moment, Sam felt like any other ninth-grade girl. And then again, she wasn't like any other girl; she had Down syndrome and she was a poet.

Not very many girls were both of those, Sam thought to herself.

The van pulled out and Sam caught a glimpse of Kacey in the crowd. She had taken off her jacket and the fish tattoo was there for all to see. A small crowd watched her every move as she threw down her backpack and shoved a girl in the back. The crowd formed a ring around the two girls and Kacey was yelling. There was definitely more than one way to get attention in the world.

Kacey's moment of glory, Sam thought.

John shuffled his feet and kicked at the front seat. "When are we going to get there?" he asked.

"John, I have told you five times, Dad comes home by 4:00 p.m. and we will have the van loaded and be ready to go," Mom answered. "Is your stuff all packed?"

"Yeah," John said.

Sam laughed to herself. John's backpack had been packed for a week. They were going on an adventure, after all, to a rented house at Fort Casey State Park on Whidbey Island. A neighbor down the street had been to the fort before and he told Sam and John about the tunnels and the hidden rooms that were deep within the old, concrete building. Since then, John had been researching the history of the fort and he had even made a map of the old gun installations and positions of the concrete bunkers.

John was a nut for gear and an even bigger nut for mysteries. He had packed all his spy equipment: his periscope, compass, pocketknife, and survival guide, plus, electrical tape, duct tape, rope, and bungee cords.

"Mom, he's had all his spy gear ready for a week," Sam said.

"Believe me, we're gonna need it!" John said.

"Well, I hope you packed some socks and underwear," Mom said looking in the rearview mirror and trying to catch a glimpse of John. He slunk down in his seat and disappeared into his camo jacket.

"I have all the important stuff," he said grumpily. "I hope this Brian kid likes spy stuff."

Brian was the eleven-year-old son of Dad's cousin Leanne. Sam's family was sharing the rental house for the weekend with Leanne, her two kids, and Leanne's brother Bruce. Even though Leanne and Bruce were Dad's cousins, Sam, John, and their older sister, Jenny, called them Aunt Leanne and Uncle Bruce. Sam couldn't remember the last time she had seen Aunt Leanne and Brian and Madison. They had lived in Washington D.C. for many years until recently and their dad, Uncle Tom, had been deployed to Afghanistan. Uncle Bruce lived in Seattle and they saw him more often.

The van parked in the driveway at home and Sam spotted her older sister, Jenny, walking up the street with Chestnut straining at the leash. Jenny was always plugged in to her music with her headphones on and seemed disconnected from planet earth. Her black clothes and heavy eyeliner added to the effect and gave Sam the feeling that Jenny was visiting from somewhere else.

Mom called to Jenny as she opened up the back of the van. "Could you get Chestnut's food and dog bed loaded for the trip?" Sam wasn't sure Jenny had heard her. "Jenny?" called Mom a second time.

"Got it," Jenny said. Mom hurried into the house and Jenny patted the back of the van and Chestnut jumped in.

"Boy, you are going to love this weekend trip," Sam said. "You know that, Chestnut? We are going to be near a beach all weekend!" She sat down on the back of the van next to the dog and gave her a scratch behind the ears.

"Hope she doesn't roll in something!" Jenny said and sat down next to Sam.

On their vacation last summer on Orcas Island in Puget Sound, Sam had been in charge of Chestnut while Jenny was working nearby at a summer camp. Chestnut had been happy as a clam, especially when she found a dead seagull or fish to roll in.

"Glad you're in charge of the dog this time," Sam said. "I gave her a lot of baths last summer!"

"That's because you let her off the leash, Sam." Jenny raised her eyebrows at her sister.

"How is it fair," Sam asked, "for the whole family to be on vacation and Chestnut doesn't get to be on vacation, too?"

"Dogs aren't people," Jenny said. Sam heard the tone in her sister's voice, the "I'm older and wiser than you" tone. Jenny was like Dad: she liked things explained and she liked things to go by the rules. "How'd the assembly go today?" Jenny asked.

"Good," Sam said. She told her big sister just about everything but she decided not to mention the incident with Kacey.

"People really seem to like my poem. Even Janey Evans liked it. Did you know her older brother is in the Navy?"

"Seems like a lot of people are in the military these days. I mean, Dad was; it's not like it's weird or anything." The sisters sat quietly and scratched Chestnut. "And of course, there's Uncle Alex and Aunt Leanne's husband, Tom."

Both girls knew that not a day went by that Dad didn't think about his younger brother, Alex, deployed in Afghanistan. This weekend at the mini family reunion with Dad's cousins, Uncle Alex would be missed and Aunt Leanne's husband, Tom, would too. He had returned wounded from Afghanistan two months ago and was supposed to be home by now from the VA hospital in Washington D.C.

"I don't remember Brian and Madison very well," Sam said.

"It's been a long time since we saw them. We spent a Christmas together but you were really little and I'm not sure John and Brian were born yet," Jenny said. "I heard Mom and Dad talking about Madison. They said she ran away from home once and she skips school, stuff like that. Guess it's 'cause her dad got wounded."

"You'd be upset wouldn't you, if something happened to Dad?" Sam asked her sister. She pictured Kacey and the fish tattoo and the small crowd after school and she wondered what Kacey was upset about.

"Of course I would," Jenny said. "Mom said the family is really disappointed because Uncle Tom was supposed to be home by this weekend." Sam thought about this and kept scratching Chestnut's ears. "I still think it's no fun to spend a three day weekend with a messed up cousin."

"Wow! That's kinda mean!" Sam blurted.

Sam was surprised at Jenny but, then again, she was beginning to see that the life of a teenager was full of lots of up and down feelings. Jenny was two years older than her and Sam watched her sister closely, hoping to find the answers to growing up.

"So Janey Evans liked the poem?" Jenny said. This was a total change of subject and Sam let it go.

"She also liked my boots," Sam said. She stuck her feet up and the sisters glanced down at the brown ankle boots with burnished buckles.

"Sweet!" Jenny said, "Too bad they aren't black!"

Sam smirked at her. Jenny loved everything black.

At that moment, Dad's car pulled into the driveway. Chestnut jumped down and ran around to greet Dad as he climbed out of the car and swung his backpack over his shoulder.

"Ready to go?" he asked.

"Yep," Jenny replied and Sam nodded.

"Let's load up, then!"

Jenny and Sam moved off the tailgate and followed Dad into the house. He held the screen door open for them and put his arm around Sam's shoulder as she came in to the kitchen.

"How did it go today?" Dad asked.

"It was the best, Dad, really the best," Sam said as she glanced up at him. If there was one person on the planet whose opinion mattered to her, it was Dad's.

"I knew you could do it!" Dad said. He gave her a hug and hurried into the house.

"We're leaving in fifteen minutes," he yelled.

Sam hurried up to her room and went to her travel bag. She had packed yesterday but now she looked around for her art supplies and paper. Sam never traveled without her journal and she loved to pack her art stuff when they went on trips. Art and writing were her favorite things to do. They were her escape. It occurred to her that she was just like Jenny that way, even she could disconnect from planet earth.

"Don't forget your toothbrushes everybody and pack your swimsuits, I think there is a pool at the park," Mom yelled to them.

"Are you crazy?" John answered, "It's only May!"

"I'm loading the kayak right now," Dad said. "Told Bruce I'd bring it and a football!" And with that, Dad headed down the steps with a duffle bag over his shoulder.

"It's gonna be freezing!" John shouted after him and trudged down the stairs dragging his big backpack.

"Supposed to be in the mid 60s and blue skies," Dad said over his shoulder.

The family converged on the driveway and loaded their stuff. Dad went back in and helped Mom bring out bags of groceries and a cooler. She paused at the back door.

"Got everything?" she asked.

"I'm good," Sam called out. Mom locked the door and loaded the last bag of supplies into the van. She got into the passenger seat and looked back at Sam, John, and Jenny.

"Where is the Chestnut?" At the sound of her name, the big dog lifted her head off of Jenny's lap in the far back seat of the van. "All accounted for," Mom said to Dad.

"Blast off!" Dad said and the family began their Memorial Day weekend.

From Sam's Top Secret Journal:

I drew a picture of Kacey Farmer's tattoo. The fish is beautiful, it has a long flowing tail and it's gold and orange. I remember the day she came to school with it. Everybody stood around her while she told us that it had a special meaning. She said that in Japan, the koi is a symbol of perseverance, (I just asked Jenny how to spell that), and strength.

I don't see how you can talk about symbols of good things and be mean at the same time. Maybe the fish isn't a koi, maybe it's a piranha (had to ask Jenny how to spell that, too!).

Today was cool! Even with Kacey doing her thing. I'm going to remember the good parts of this day.

CHAPTER 2

The "Valor" Meal

"I'm hungry," John said.

Sam looked up from her journal and out the van window at the slow snake of cars winding down the freeway. They had been bogged down in traffic for over an hour.

"Jenny," Mom lowered her passenger visor and looked in the mirror trying to catch Jenny's eye. As usual, Jenny was lost in her music and sitting back with her eyes closed, her lips slightly moving and oblivious to the world.

"Jenny," Sam reached around and hit Jenny's knee. Jenny's eyes opened sleepily and she pulled one side of her headphones off to hear.

"Hmm?"

"Honey, grab a cheese stick out of the cooler for John," Mom said.

"I don't want a cheese stick, I want dinner," he said.

They were all silent for a moment. Sam knew what he meant. They had barely reached the outskirts of Seattle and were still an hour away from the ferry dock at Mukilteo and the boat to Whidbey Island.

"Rick's Drive-in!" Dad yelled.

"No way!" John said.

Sam and Jenny looked at each other with big eyes. Dad never took them out for junk food. Only on rare occasions did the family get such a treat, but Rick's had a special place in Dad's heart and his stomach. Dad and Uncle Alex always made it a point to eat at Rick's when Dad's brother was home from deployment. Uncle Alex said he dreamt about Rick's burgers, fries, and shakes from the mountains of Afghanistan and the deserts of Iraq.

"In honor of Uncle Alex!" Dad said and he smiled at Mom as he veered off the freeway.

"Burger, fries, shake, burger, fries, shake, burger, fries, shake," John chanted.

Rick's Drive-in was famous for its handmade shakes and everyone in the family always had one: strawberry for Jenny, vanilla for Mom and chocolate for Sam, John, and Dad. John's chant was the truth. Burger, fries, shake.

Chestnut sat up in the back seat as they pulled into the parking lot and sniffed the air. A thin line of blue smoke trailed out of the big vent on the top of the drive-in and the smell of grilled burgers and hot oil and French fries flooded the van as Sam, John, and Dad opened the doors and stepped out.

Chestnut whined and licked her chops.

"Don't forget ketchup," Jenny said without opening her eyes.

Rick's Drive-in was built in the '60s and had a sleek, retro look. Stainless steel counters wrapped around a wall of glass windows and the customers could see everything going on inside the drive-in. Workers wore orange T-shirts and aprons moved at lightning speed to serve up Rick's famous burgers.

Sam, John, and Dad stood in a long line but it moved quickly, and in a moment Dad was bent down and giving the order through a small opening in the big glass window. John collected straws out of the dispenser.

"What'll it be?" a girl asked. Sam could see by her name tag that she went by Polly.

"We'd like five burgers, five fries, three chocolate shakes, one vanilla and one strawberry, please," Dad said. "And five ketchups."

Polly disappeared and joined the flurry of workers stuffing bags with hamburgers and reaching in the freezer for the shakes.

"Look," Sam said. She pointed to a hand lettered sign to the side of the little order window.

"Memorial Weekend Special: Free shake with every meal for vets and military personnel. Thank you for your service and valor. With ID please."

"That's you, Dad," she said. Sam nudged Dad and pointed to the sign as he fumbled with his wallet. Dad had been in the Air Force and the military had helped him with medical school. He was now a surgeon in Seattle and she was so proud of him.

"Sixteen dollars and forty-two cents," the girl behind the counter said. She passed two bags of fries and burgers and the cardboard tray of shakes out of the sliding window.

"I didn't see this sign until just now," Dad said. He stepped back from the window and pointed to the small sign. "I'm a vet." He showed the girl his veteran's ID card.

"So?" she said.

Dad pointed to the sign again and the girl stuck her head out the window to try and read it.

"I'm sorry, I can't see it," Polly's tone was exasperated. "Hey, what does this sign say?" the girl called into the workspace as she pointed to the backside of the sign.

Sam felt the line of waiting customers behind her shuffle and shift impatiently. The other workers looked at the girl but didn't offer any help until a tall, skinny boy hurried behind her. Sam saw the word "manager" on his name tag in bold letters above the name "Aaron".

"It's a special for veterans and military in honor of Memorial Day," Aaron said. "Free shake with a meal." He brushed past the girl and opened the next small order window. "May I help the next customer, please?" Aaron called out. The line behind Sam moved to the new window.

The girl pursed her lips and blew air up to her bangs that hung down from the brown cap with its logo, "Rick's: Voted Best Fries 2013". There was sweat on her forehead and a big splotch of grease on her short, orange apron. Sam watched in amazement as the girl's fingers flew over the cash register and she re-calculated the total.

"My grandpa was in Vietnam." She said this matter-of-factly and then let out another long sigh. "Fourteen, seventy-eight," she said to Dad. "More fries!" she yelled over her shoulder to someone working at the back. She quickly gave Dad his change and pushed the bags of food out of the way and looked beyond Dad to the next customer. "Next?"

Sam grabbed a big wad of paper napkins and one of the bags, John grabbed the other, and Dad juggled the tray of shakes. Mom reached across the van and opened Dad's door as he slid in balancing the drinks. Sam and John climbed in the back and took their food and passed the bag to Jenny.

"Burger, shakes, fries," John chanted. "Burgers, shakes, fries!"

"Chill, John," Jenny said.

"Dad got a free shake," Sam said.

"For what?" Jenny asked. Her older sister had re-entered the land of the living when the smell of their dinner filled the car. Chestnut whined and wiggled. Sam knew that Jenny would feed the dog a French fry or two.

"For valor," John said as he folded open the paper on his burger and took a huge bite. "Whatever that means."

"Don't talk with your mouth full," Mom said to him.

"Special discount for vets and military," Dad said and with that, he held up his milkshake. "A toast to Uncle Alex and Uncle Tom!" The rest of the family held up their shakes and toasted.

"To Uncle Alex and Uncle Tom!" they yelled.

The car immediately grew quiet as the family munched happily. John slurped his chocolate shake.

"What is valor, anyway?" he asked.

"It's when people are brave," Jenny said from the back seat.

"People are brave all the time," John said. "Remember Mr. Wilkins?"

Sam thought about their neighbor back in Florida. Mr. Wilkin's house had caught on fire and he had escaped but ran back inside to save his old cat, Nicky. He became a local hero and he and Nicky had their picture on the front page of the paper.

"He's not as brave as Uncle Alex," Sam said. Certainly what her uncle was doing in Afghanistan showed more bravery than rescuing a cat. Being in the Army was about valor but it probably wouldn't get your picture in the paper.

"It takes a certain kind of courage to be in the military," Mom added.

It seemed to Sam that courage and valor were everywhere. Even this afternoon, Mom had told Sam that she thought she was brave for reading her poem.

'Thanks, Dad," Sam said. She reached around and touched his arm.

"You're welcome. It's great to eat a burger once in a while," Dad said stuffing some fries into his mouth.

"No, I mean for your valor," Sam said.

"I was just doing my job," Dad said. He seemed to brush off the idea but Sam sensed he was embarrassed or maybe she should have been quiet about Uncle Alex.

What they do is more than just a job, Sam thought.

She looked through the car window to the stressed-out girl in her dirty orange T-shirt and brown hat.

Maybe Polly has a kind of valor, too, Sam thought.

"Hey, Dad got a SUPER VALOR MEAL," John said.

"That's enough," Dad said. He handed his trash to Mom, put his unfinished shake in the cup holder between the seats, and said, "Buckle up! We're outta here!"

☆ ☆ ☆

The freeway had cleared so they drove to the ferry in good time. They quickly boarded the gigantic boat and departed across beautiful Puget Sound. On the other side of the passage, the Olympic Mountains stood in all their glory against the deepening pink sky.

"So beautiful," Mom said.

"You promised that we could check out the fort tonight," John said. He leaned forward and talked directly to Dad.

"Yep," Dad answered, "that I did. Let's see if the daylight holds out for us."

John sat back and stared out at the sky; it was growing darker by the second. It didn't help that the highway entered a tall canyon of evergreen trees and Dad flipped on the headlights. Sam gave up hope but John pressed his nose against the window and craned his neck to see the pink ribbon of sky above the trees.

"It's still light!" he said.

"I think we're going to make it," Dad laughed.

Dad drove for a while and then followed a sign and turned into the park on a narrow road and through a gate.

"There's a sign on the gate that says the park closes at dusk," Sam said.

"Gate's still open," John said.

They pulled into the empty parking lot and got out.

Across a large lawn, Fort Casey stood abandoned and menacing in the darkening sky. The huge concrete bunker was built into the hillside and only rusty, metal staircases and doors faced them. Far to the right and built on a bluff, a lighthouse stood tall and still like a pale ghost.

"Scary" Sam said.

"Cool!" John said.

He leapt out of the van and took off running with Sam, Jenny, and Chestnut right behind him.

"Just watch your step!" Dad yelled.

Sam and John hurried up a metal staircase to the top of the fort. Sam felt like she was standing on top of the world. The vast concrete building was level to the ground and they stood at the edge of a cliff to the beach. They looked out over the water that reflected the colorful sunset. The fort didn't seem so scary on top.

"That's the Admiralty Lighthouse," John said. He pointed to the building that gleamed pale pink in the brilliant sunset.

He bolted toward a huge hole in the concrete where a cannon was housed beneath the ground. There was a short set of concrete stairs and he went down into the gun placement.

"Look, Dad," he yelled.

Mom and Dad came up behind them.

"That's one big gun," Mom said.

"You know they never used these guns. They were left over from WWI and they were never used here. No enemies ever entered into Puget Sound," John explained.

"That's a lot of concrete for nothing," Sam said. "Look at that view, they should build houses here!"

"No way!" John said.

He climbed out of the gun placement.

"We better get out of here before the park ranger locks us in," Dad said.

"Aw!"

"We have all weekend to explore," Dad said.

John scurried back down the metal steps and the family followed. Jenny was waiting patiently at the bottom of the stairs with Chestnut.

"You have to see the killer sunset," Mom said to Jenny. "I'll take Chestnut." Mom took the leash and watched Jenny hurry up the metal stairs. John was dragging open one of the big metal doors and it screeched and screamed against the concrete sidewalk.

"John, back to the car" Mom sighed. She turned and headed toward the parking lot. As Mom and Dad walked away, John ducked quietly through the door. Sam watched then saw the glow of his flashlight.

Leave it to John to have the right gear, she thought.

Sam snuck in behind him but the moment she walked in, John turned off the flashlight.

"Boo!" John yelled.

Sam stopped in the dark concrete room and John quickly switched the light back on and looked intently at his sister.

"Got ya!" he said. To his surprise, she gave him a big smile and started to laugh.

"Takes more than that to scare me," Sam said.

"Since when?" he asked.

"Since today!" Sam said.

And with that they walked out and headed for the van. Sam turned around to look at the gorgeous sunset one last time.

This has been a super day, Sam thought and turned to catch up with her family.

From Sam's Top Secret Journal:

We made it to Whidbey! Mom and Dad have rented the coolest big old house. It was officer's quarters a long time ago; it's enormous! Leanne and Bruce and their kids arrive tomorrow morning so we had first pick of the bedrooms. Jenny and I have to share but Jenny said it was okay, as long as she didn't have to share with Madison. John will share with Brian.

Jenny and I flipped a coin to see who got the bed by the big window. I won! She said you could see all the way to Japan from here.

We arrived right at sunset but John wouldn't let Dad forget his promise to take us over to Fort Casey for a quick look. You can walk there from this house.

It is a huge concrete building, long and low and scary looking. I was glad that Dad was there. John flipped out he thought it was so cool. He can't wait to get back with his spy gear and his maps.

Tomorrow will be fun! I am sort of anxious about seeing my cousins. It's been a long time; I don't feel like I know them at all.

CHAPTER 3

Family

The smell of cinnamon rolls and the sound of seagulls woke Sam up from her Saturday morning sleep.

Whidbey Island!

She reached over the edge of the bed and picked up her glasses. Jenny was already up and gone and Sam left her cozy covers to look out the window.

The officer's house they had rented was built on a small hill and Sam looked out across the big field that stretched to the beach and the woods on the far side. Beyond the woods was the fort they had visited last night. In the daylight, she could see the top of the Admiralty Lighthouse sticking above the trees and mountaintops in the distance.

Sam pulled on her jeans and a T-shirt and slipped into her boots. In the bathroom, she brushed her teeth and splashed some water on her face. She brushed her long, shiny, straight hair and pushed it all to one side over her shoulder and dropped her arms to her sides. Before her, she saw a strong, medium-build girl with perfect skin and light brown hair that cascaded onto the big smily face on her T-shirt. She smiled at herself and turned and went downstairs.

"Here's the sleepy head!" Mom said when Sam walked into the kitchen. "Cinnamon rolls!"

Mom and Dad sat in front of steaming cups of coffee and cinnamon rolls the size of dinner plates. Dad was crazy about homemade pie and cinnamon rolls. Sam and Jenny joked that the family's vacations were planned around the best places to buy them.

"Dad could write a book, "*A Hungry Man's Guide to the Best Pies and Cinnamon Rolls of the Northwest*"," Mom said.

John sat in front of an empty plate and Sam noticed his backpack on the floor by his chair. He drummed his fingers on the tabletop.

"John," Dad said without looking up at him, "I'm going to eat this cinnamon roll in peace. Go outside, we'll go to the fort as soon as Leanne and Bruce get here, then we can take the cousins with us."

"Aw, Dad," John said. He slumped and twisted in his chair and stood up and pushed it against the table and slouched out of the kitchen dragging his backpack.

"Here you go, honey," Mom said. She set a roll in front of Sam and stopped to run her hand down Sam's long ponytail. "Sleep well?"

"Jenny snores," Sam said. "But yeah, I slept like a rock!"

"That's good. You had a big day yesterday."

Sam started to smear the icing over the hot cinnamon roll with her finger when she heard stomping coming up the front steps. She popped her finger into her mouth just before Chestnut hurried into the kitchen and put her head in Sam's lap. The dog was cold and smelled like the out-of-doors. She snuffled Sam with her wet nose.

"Ewww," Sam said. She pushed the dog's head away. Chestnut moved down the table towards Dad.

"They're here!" Jenny said and set the dog leash on the counter.

"Bruce and Leanne?" Mom asked.

"Leanne and her kids."

Dad and Sam each took a huge bite of their cinnamon rolls. Icing dribbled down the corners of his mouth and Sam had the delicious, sticky glaze all over her fingers again. They looked at each other and laughed with their mouths full.

"Come on, you two!" Mom said as she dried her hands on a dishtowel and went out.

"You're here, you're here!" Mom said to the cousins. Chestnut barked.

"Wow, cool dog!" said the voice of a young boy.

"This is Chestnut!" Mom exclaimed. "She's friendly."

Sam and Dad got up from the table and came out into the hallway. Sam stood behind Dad as he hugged his cousin, Leanne.

"You remember, Brian," she said.

Brian had been kneeling down and petting Chestnut. He stood up and shook Dad's hand.

"Hey, there," Dad said with a big grin.

"And, Madison," Leanne continued.

All eyes turned to Madison who stood halfway in and halfway out of the front door. She was hunched over with her arms across her chest and seemed to hide under her bangs that were dyed bright red. In contrast, her long black hair straggled down the sides of her face. She looked tired and nervous. For a second, Sam was reminded of Polly from Rick's Drive-in.

"Hey, there, Madison." Dad reached out to shake her hand but she didn't move and he gave her an awkward wave and stepped back. "Good to see you again."

"You all remember, Sam," Dad said. He moved back and put his arm around Sam's shoulders. Sam was embarrassed by the attention and wished she could disappear into the woodwork but instead she shook hands with everyone except with Madison who still stood with her arms folded.

"Coffee and cinnamon rolls in the kitchen," Mom said.

"Madison and Brian, go grab the stuff out of the van. Madison, the cooler can go in the kitchen. Where are they going to sleep?" Leanne looked at Mom.

"You can choose upstairs or down," Mom said. "Maybe Brian and John could share?"

"Cool," Brian said.

"There is a small room at the back of this floor that is perfect for one person," Jenny said to Madison. "You could have one to yourself!"

"Whatever," Madison shrugged. She backed out the screened door and turned on her heel. Jenny followed after her.

"I'll help bring stuff in," Jenny said to Aunt Leanne.

"Lovely girl!" Aunt Leanne said to Dad. "At least she speaks more than one word." She shook her head. "Coffee sounds great."

Sam followed the her parents and Aunt Leanne back into the kitchen and they all sat down. Sam could easily see that Dad and Leanne were first cousins. They both looked like Sam's grandma, slender, with golden brown hair, big eyes, and an easy grin.

"How is Tom?" Mom asked.

"He is doing great. He was being released this week," Leanne said. Leanne's husband had spent the last month in a VA hospital in Washington, D.C. getting special therapy. "You know how it goes with the military, a lot of red tape," she said. "Next week, I hope. I can't believe we will all be together again. It's been a month since I visited him there the last time. A whole month, but I just can't get away with the kids in school and all. And my work."

Madison and Jenny walked into the kitchen. Madison carried a small backpack and Jenny lugged a cooler.

"Straight back," Jenny said. She nodded toward the downstairs bedrooms as she set down the cooler and started to unload it into the refrigerator. Madison disappeared down the hallway and they heard a door slam.

"Don't do that, Jenny," Leanne interrupted her. "That's Madison's job."

John and Brian burst into the kitchen.

"Dad," John said. "How 'bout we get a head start to the fort? We will wait for you on the lawn in front. We won't go in, we promise!"

"Okay with you, Leanne?"

"Sounds great, have fun!"

Leanne smiled at the boys as Madison appeared in the kitchen.

"Maddie, unload the cooler into the refrigerator, would you please?" Aunt Leanne asked.

"I'm going to the beach," she said and walked out of the room.

The defiance in her voice left a chill in the warm kitchen. Sam stopped chewing and looked at Dad and Mom. Aunt Leanne's gaze followed her daughter out of the room and she started to say something but stopped and took a sip of coffee instead.

"I got it, Aunt Leanne," Jenny chimed in. "No biggie."

Jenny tackled the chore as they heard the front door slam.

"She's upset about her dad," Aunt Leanne said. Her voice was sad and tired. "We have all had to do extra without him at home and now, well, the kids don't know how it will be. Nobody does. Maddie loves her dad more than anything."

"Tom's a brave soldier, she can be proud of him for that," Dad offered.

"Oh, I think she is, but you know, now Tom is impaired and nobody knows what his progress will be. You know how teenagers are, they don't want to be different," Aunt Leanne stopped.

Sam knew that one, being different.

"And Madison had her heart set on seeing him this weekend," Aunt Leanne said.

"Any day now, I bet," Dad said.

The grown-ups were quiet while they sipped their coffee until Jenny interrupted their silence.

"Come on, squirt," she said to Sam. She had finished unloading the cooler and grabbed a banana from the kitchen table. "Let's see if we can't find Madison and then catch up with John and Brian. Meet you guys at the main entrance to the fort."

"Why don't you go ahead and explore the fort?" Dad said looking at his watch. "If we don't catch up with you in an hour, we'll meet you at the lighthouse museum. Bruce can see the fort later. I am counting on you to be in charge, Jenny."

"As long as Chestnut stays with you?" Jenny asked.

"Sure," Mom said.

The girls hurried out of the house into the sunny day and Jenny took off running.

"Wait up!" Sam called.

Jenny was jogging across the field and Sam couldn't keep up. When she ran, her gait was weird and it was hard not to feel awkward and off balance.

"Wait!" she called again.

Jenny stopped and Sam caught up with her.

"I hate this," Jenny said.

"What?"

"This!" Jenny waved her arms in the direction of Madison. "Chasing after some ballistic girl," Jenny said. "This is exactly what I didn't want to do this weekend!"

"Then why are we doing it?" Sam asked. She guessed that ballistic was another word for crazy. She was about to ask Jenny when Jenny started in again.

"You know Mom will just make us be nice," Jenny said. She bent over to pick a piece of tall grass, stuck the end in her mouth and chewed on it. "She'll make us be with her anyway."

"Mmm," Sam agreed. She copied her sister and reached down and grabbed a piece of grass. The two girls stood in the sunshine and looked after Madison.

Jenny was right. Mom had a thing about accepting everybody and Sam understood this better than Jenny. Sam wanted people to accept her and her DS and she knew that it meant following the Golden Rule, or at least trying to be kind to others.

There was a time when she was little that Sam wanted to be everyone's friend but she learned that wasn't possible. Her sister was a really good person but she kept her distance and she always talked to Sam about having good boundaries. Now that Sam was older, she realized that friends were special people and not everyone was nice. Sometimes her DS made it hard to tell the difference between sincere people and not nice people.

"*Boo!*" Kacey Farmer's voice echoed in her mind. Sam knew it was true; sometimes people were mean.

"Oh, let's go," Jenny sighed.

Jenny didn't run this time and they managed to catch up with Madison. She barely glanced up when they reached her but instead, she stood bent over her cell phone, her red bangs hanging like a velvet curtain over her face.

Sam stared jealously at the red bangs. Since last fall, she had begged Mom to let her put a green or purple stripe underneath the back of her long brown hair. Her best friend Abby had been allowed to do it. Sam had explained this to Mom many times.

"You won't even see it," Sam said. "It will be underneath in the back!"

"What's the point then?" Mom asked.

"I just wanna be like my friends. It would only show a little when I wore my hair up."

"You're not Abby" Mom said.

Sam couldn't help but admire the red bangs. Madison raised her head and her big blue eyes were opened wide in disbelief.

"There's no frigging reception here!" Madison held the phone up as though it were a useless thing that she was going to throw away but she shoved it into her back pocket.

"We are sort of in the middle of nowhere," Sam offered.

"Duh," Madison said as she shivered and hunched over. She had no socks on and the toes of her tennis shoes had holes in them and were completely soaked from the dew on the grass.

"The fort is this way," Jenny said and started off toward the woods.

"I'm going to the beach," Madison said and turned and walked away. "Maybe there's some reception down there!"

Sam started after her but Jenny grabbed her arm.

"Let's go to the fort and find John and Brian," she said.

CHAPTER 4

Dark Dungeons and Sunny Cliffs

The two sisters followed the trail to the fort through the woods. The sun was heating up the forest floor and a sweet smell like Christmas trees filled the warm air. Except for a few bird chirps, there was only the sound of their footsteps thumping softly on the thick carpet of pine needles.

"She's not very friendly," Sam said.

"You can say that again," Jenny said.

"I like her hair," Sam said. "I wish Mom would let me dye my bangs!"

Jenny stopped on the trail and turned to her sister.

"Your hair looks great just the way it is," Jenny said.

"Now, you sound like Mom," Sam said.

Jenny held up a piece of her hair. The ends of Jenny's hair were dyed black.

"I had to wait until I was sixteen. You're fourteen!"

And with that, Jenny turned and kept hiking. Sam kicked a small rock on the pathway.

The sisters emerged from the woods and crossed the parking lot. In the bright sunshine, the fort looked old, not scary like it had the night before. Sam spotted John and Brian sitting cross-legged at the edge of the big concrete area that surrounded the fort. They were looking at a map that John had made of the old gun placements.

"Hey, you guys," Jenny called. "You ready to go take a look?"

"Where's Dad?" John asked.

"Waiting for Uncle Bruce. They'll be along or we'll meet them at the lighthouse museum," Jenny said.

John and Brian stuffed the map back into the backpack and started to the fort. They climbed a different set of steps today. Large concrete stairways went up from ground level to the upper deck of the fort. Some of the stairs stopped midway up the concrete bunkers and an even steeper metal stairway finished the climb to the top.

The concrete top of the fort gave way to forty feet of mowed lawn that extended to the edge of the bluff. A big sign read, "No Beach Access." Sam walked across the grass and looked over the edge. It was a long ways down. She saw the faint outline of a zigzagging path all the way down to the beach. It was obvious that some people had disobeyed the sign. In fact, Sam could see the outline of someone at the bottom of the cliff.

"To the cannon!" John yelled.

"No running!" Jenny called after the boys. Jenny stood next to Sam looking out at the view and then down the cliff. "Wow! I wouldn't want to try that."

"Looks like somebody is," Sam said. The girls stared down the long hill for a second. Sure enough, someone was climbing up the steep trail.

"Crazy," Jenny said and they went to find the boys.

There were signs posted all over the top of the fort that said to watch your step. Thick lines of yellow paint outlined the sheer drop-offs at the face of the fort and along the edges of the stairwells and gun batteries. There were no hand or guardrails on top of the fort as they could be seen from the water. Sam wondered how the soldiers had managed to move quickly without falling into a stairwell or off the drop-offs.

John and Brian were at the cannon that they had explored the night before. The gun pointed at an angle into the air and it was possible to shimmy out to the end of the gun barrel. If you were tall enough you could climb up into the gunner's seat and out onto the gun and straddle it. Little kids sat on the lower end of the gun held by their parents' outstretched arms.

John dropped his backpack and he and Brian took their turns moving out to the very end of the gun. They waved at Jenny and Sam.

"Hey, look!" Brian yelled. He pointed over the edge of the cliff and Sam and Jenny turned.

At first, Sam couldn't see what Brian was pointing to, but a moment later, two pale arms reached over the edge of the steep cliff and Madison's red bangs popped up. The small crowd had turned to look and there was a hush as they all watched the skinny girl climb over the edge of the cliff and onto the lawn.

Madison stood up and stared back over the edge. John and Brian swung down from the cannon and joined Jenny and Sam where Madison stood. She was crying.

"Are you crazy?" her brother asked.

"I dropped my phone on the way up. I can't believe it; I dropped my phone," she moaned.

"This isn't the way up," Brian continued. "You are supposed to come up that way!" Brian pointed off in the distance beyond the field to the beach trails.

"I was taking a shortcut," Madison sniffled.

The cousins looked over the edge of the cliff. Waves crashed against the driftwood below. It would be impossible to get back down or find a phone.

"I'm going back down," Madison said. Before they could say anything, she sat down on the grass and started to scoot over to the edge.

"Stop!"

A big voice boomed from behind Sam and she looked to see a park ranger moving toward Madison.

"Step away from the cliff."

The ranger was calm almost friendly, he stopped and stood by Madison waiting for her to follow his directions. Sam figured he didn't know that Madison wasn't one for taking directions.

"My phone!" she said sadly and pointed down the cliff.

"I'm sure it's long gone. There's no way you can go back down there," he said. Madison didn't get up right away and the ranger stood patiently. She scooted back and stood up. "Thanks! Stay off the cliff." And he walked away.

"Mom's gonna kill you," Brian said.

Madison didn't say anything but brushed herself off.

"I could've done it. My phone is down there!"

Brian shook his head and started to say something.

"Forget it!" John said. "Let's go check out a dungeon." He handed Brian the backpack and they walked off toward the nearest stairwell and disappeared down the steep stairs.

"Let's climb out the gun barrel," Jenny said. "You up for it, Sam?"

"For sure!"

Sam and Jenny took the steps down into the gun placement. There were quite a few people at the fort now and they waited their turn to climb up onto the gunner's seat. From there, they straddled the barrel and worked their way out to the end of the gun where they could see the magnificent view. Sam looked down to see the steep trail that Madison had climbed.

Her view was broken by Madison walking directly in front of her, balancing on the edge of the concrete wall of the gun placement and walking slowly, one foot in front of the other on the yellow warning line painted on the edge of the concrete.

"You better be careful, Madison," Jenny yelled.

Madison ignored Jenny and continued to walk with her arms outstretched for balance. People stepped out of her way and turned to watch her.

"I'm getting down," Jenny said.

She swung down and held herself by her arms on the gun barrel and then dropped to her feet. Sam stared down for a minute. She was used to heights because she rock climbed every week at Vertical Limit but she paused to gauge the distance before she imitated Jenny and swung down.

Both girls looked up from the bottom of the gun placement to where Madison stood.

"No!" Sam exclaimed. She took a sharp intake of breath and grabbed Jenny's arm and pointed above them. Madison leaned over the edge, grabbed the end of the gun and then vaulted off the yellow line with both feet and straddled the barrel, landing perfectly. She sat facing other kids who were shimmying their way out to the end of the gun.

"Jeez! Madison," Jenny yelled at her.

The skinny girl kept moving toward the others on the gun forcing them to scoot backward and make way for her.

"Beep, beep!" she said.

"Hey, you can't do that!" A parent reached up and grabbed a little boy from off the big gun and the boy began to cry. The parent eyed Madison angrily. "You need to take turns like everyone else!" the parent said.

Madison didn't say anything but climbed down from the gun as people stepped aside making room for her.

She tossed her head and Sam saw the look on her face, the same look that was on Kacey's face at the assembly yesterday.

It was a look that said, "*I don't care.*"

"Really?" Jenny walked up to her cousin. "You think that's any way to behave in front of little kids?"

"Big deal," she said tossing her red bangs. She brought her fingers to her mouth and chewed on a fingernail, not looking Jenny in the eye. "They'll get their turn."

"You think you can just do whatever you want, don't you?" Jenny asked. She stood tall in front of Madison and Sam thought her sister looked a little scary. Her dark eyeliner and black T-shirt made her look tough but Sam knew her sister had the biggest heart in the world and probably cared too much about everything.

"It's a free world," Madison said and turned to walk away. "I'll do what I want."

Sam pulled on her sister's sleeve but Jenny jerked her arm away.

"I hate it when people are mean" Jenny said under her breath.

"Nobody got hurt," Sam said. She was still amazed how Madison had climbed the steep cliff and then vaulted onto the end of the cannon.

"She's crazy," Jenny said.

"Come on," Sam said.

The girls walked over to the stairwell. In the distance, they saw Madison crossing the field and meeting up with Dad and Aunt Leanne, Mom and Chestnut.

"Is that Uncle Bruce?" Jenny asked.

"Uncle Bruce!" Sam yelled.

She and Jenny rushed down the stairs and started across the field when Sam stopped.

"Did you hear that?"

Jenny stopped and they both listened. A muffled yelling and banging came from behind a huge metal door at the bottom of the stairwell.

"Help! Help!"

Jenny and Sam looked at each other.

"John?" The girls asked each other at the same time.

The yells came from behind a huge, rusty door that was built flush into the thick concrete. The handle was welded open but an old piece of chain hung from a broken door handle. Someone had looped the chain over a hook in the concrete wall and the door was tightly shut.

Jenny went to the door, unhooked the link of chain, and yanked hard on the heavy door.

John and Brian spilled out of the concrete dungeon.

"I'm gonna kill her," Brian said. "Where is she?"

John grabbed Brian's arm and in his other hand he held a flashlight.

"Maybe it wasn't her," John said.

"Yeah, right!"

Brian spotted his sister across the field with the grown-ups and he stopped.

"Hey," John said, "it worked out okay. We had everything we needed!"

"What would've happened if we hadn't come down here?" Sam asked.

"I have water and granola bars and extra batteries!" John said. "We could've lasted a couple of days!"

Sam laughed at her brother; he was always happy when he got a chance to use his gear.

"Yeah," Brian said. He turned his attention to John. "That was pretty cool. You guys should see this."

Brian and John went back to the door but didn't step too far in. Sam and Jenny looked over them as John shined his flashlight around the room. The concrete dungeon was dark and damp, a puddle of water filled the corner, and large shelves built into the concrete were empty. There was no light and no window. Sam was glad she hadn't been trapped in there even if John had a flashlight.

"Creepy," Jenny said.

"I'm not gonna give Madison the satisfaction of saying anything," Brian said as he backed out of the door. "She just wants the attention. That's all she ever wants, even if it's bad attention."

"Yeah," said John, "we had it handled."

Sam looked at Jenny and wondered if she was as willing as Brian to let Madison go.

"Maybe you two are right. Maybe ignoring her is the way to go," Jenny said. "Let's go see Uncle Bruce!"

With that, the four of them hurried to join their family on the trail to the Admiralty Head Lighthouse.

"Uncle Bruce!" the girls screamed.

A tall, athletic man stopped and opened his arms and grinned. The girls threw their arms around their favorite uncle. Uncle Bruce was Leanne's brother and like an older brother to Dad and Uncle Alex. He often spent Christmas with Sam's family but they rarely saw him otherwise. He was a scientist who worked with the World Health Organization and he traveled a lot with his work. He had a successful career but no wife or family of his own. The best thing about Uncle Bruce was his sense of humor and his guitar!

"Whoa, the both of you, all grown up!" he said. He stepped back to look at Jenny and Sam. "And you, too, Madison. How've you been?"

"She takes after you," Aunt Leanne chimed in. "She sang a solo at the school concert!"

"That's my girl!" Bruce grinned.

Madison smiled at the praise. "Did you bring your guitar, Uncle Bruce?" she asked. She dropped her arms and stood up straight. For a second, Sam thought she looked pretty.

"Sure did!" he said. "Guess we'll all have to sing after dinner tonight!"

He winked at Madison.

"Some of you, maybe," Mom said.

Sam felt another twinge of envy. Uncle Bruce played the guitar and sang and everyone loved it when he brought his guitar out but in Sam's family, no one could sing or play a lick. They couldn't even manage a decent Happy Birthday or a Christmas carol. They all loved to clap and participate but they left the singing to others.

"Hey, how was the fort?" Mom asked.

Jenny and Sam looked at the boys and Madison paused on the trail. Brian smiled at John.

"Totally cool," Brian said. "Great view from up there and we climbed on the old gun. John had flashlights and we checked out one of the dungeons."

"Yeah, it was great!" John nodded.

Sam watched Madison for a reaction. The boys were ignoring her and Sam saw her smile dim as she hunched her shoulders. Brian had his sister figured out.

"What do you know about this museum, John?" Uncle Bruce asked.

"Did you know it was built in 1914?" John asked. Before Uncle Bruce could answer, he began sharing his information and he and Brian and Uncle Bruce huddled together as they walked quickly toward the old lighthouse. Uncle Bruce looked back and winked at the girls.

There was a reason he was everyone's favorite uncle. He cared!

CHAPTER 5

Lighthouses and Red Poppies

In the window of the front door to the Admiralty Lighthouse and Museum, there was a handmade sign:

"Remembering the Fallen: A Memorial Day Exhibit."
Special Museum Hours: Fri.-Mon. Memorial Day Weekend

"Look, Dad," John said. "Bound to have some war memorabilia!"

John was an expert on the military and he was always on the lookout for medals or hats or parts of uniforms. He kept his collection in a display case in his room. In the case was his favorite present of all time! It was a huge book that showed all the military medals from all the branches of the United States Armed Forces and many foreign countries, too. Uncle Bruce had given it to him for Christmas a few years ago.

The family paid their admission and entered the dim, cool museum gallery.

"No backpacks allowed," A man in a security uniform put his arm up in front of John. "You need to check that, son."

"Aw," John grumbled.

If there was one thing John didn't like it was being separated from his backpack. He walked off to check it at the front desk of the museum.

"Whoa, cool," John said as he entered the museum gallery. Sam saw that his disappointment about the backpack was immediately forgotten when he saw the many exhibits.

The walls of the main room were covered with enlarged photos of the original lighthouse as it had looked when it was still a working lighthouse. In this very room, the keeper of the lighthouse lived with his family. Almost everything in the enlarged picture was on display in the museum: furniture, rugs, a globe, maps, and artwork; everything but the people and family who had once worked and lived there.

In the middle of the room, surrounded by a heavy gold cord, was the original lens from the lighthouse tower. It was four feet tall and looked like a huge pinecone made of clear, thick glass. The cut glass lens worked to magnify a small light to create the strong bright beam that shone out over the waters of Puget Sound.

Sam went into the next room and found John and Brian huddled over a display case. In it were original photos of Fort Casey when it had been an active fort and Sam saw all the big guns were in place and the soldiers who stood at the ready.

"I think this is the cannon that is still there," John said. "Look, it used to swivel all the way around."

John had a comment on just about everything and he shared his online research with Brian who was equally enthusiastic.

Sam joined Madison at a display case with books open to war scenes in Europe. Several pages showed the dead and wounded and Madison stood transfixed in front of them. Uncle Bruce came up behind her.

"I hate war," Madison said. Sam heard the word hate but Madison had said it without any feeling. "This is so messed up."

Madison tapped on the glass of the display case with her fingernail, pointing to a blurry black-and-white picture of flag-draped coffins in neat rows waiting to be loaded onto a cargo plane. The girls stood quietly looking at the grim photos and Uncle Bruce moved over to stand beside them.

"This is gross," Madison said. She looked up at Uncle Bruce, her eyes big and sad beneath the red bangs.

"Come over here and look at this painting with me," he said. Sam heard the gentle tone in his voice and she knew he was trying to distract Madison. "You, too, Sam."

They walked across the room to a large oil painting of a field of red flowers.

"How about this? Sam, you like all things to do with writing and art. Did you know that the red poppy is a symbol of all the war dead?" He turned to Madison and pointed to a plaque on the wall that explained the symbol of the red poppy.

"Yes," Sam said. "I just wrote a poem for our school's Memorial Day assembly. And when I was doing some research I ran into another poem. Something about a field somewhere."

Madison looked irritated that Sam had the answer, and now, it was Sam's turn to beam.

"That's it," Bruce said. 'In Flanders Field.' I guess there is a poem for everything. What was your poem about?"

"I called it, 'Remembering'," Sam said. In a soft voice, she recited the poem.

"Wow, great words!" Uncle Bruce said and pretended to clap his hands together in applause.

"My dad didn't die," Madison said. "He just got messed up. I don't see anyone writing poems about that kinda thing." She stopped herself but as if she couldn't help it, she pointed at the painting. "The red symbolizes all the blood. That is totally freaky."

She turned and walked away and Sam and Uncle Bruce looked at each other.

"Don't mind her, Sam. She seems to have a lot on her mind." Sam wondered how Madison's dad, Uncle Tom, would be when he came back.

They joined John and Brian across the room at a little card table. Behind the cardboard table sat an elderly man with his military cap on. There were many pins and ribbons on his hat and on his lapel was pinned a red poppy. Around the room were other older men sitting in front of their displays. They were all veterans.

"Sam, look at this," John said. He moved over as Sam came up to him. "This is Mr. Merton. This is my sister, Sam."

"Nice to meet ya," he said. He gave Sam a big smile and his eyes almost disappeared in his wrinkled face. He held out a pale hand that trembled as Sam shook it.

"Mr. Merton was in World War II," John said. "Can you believe that?"

Mr. Merton laughed at John's comment. "Hah," he said, "back with the dinosaurs."

Dad came up and put his hand on John's shoulder.

"Hey, Dad, look!"

John let Dad get closer to the card table. He pointed to a medal in an open wooden case lined with a yellowed shiny fabric. The medal hung from a braided ribbon necklace.

"Look, the word *valor*," John said. "It's the Army Medal of Honor."

"This is yours, sir?" Dad asked.

The whole family was gathered now around the old man and his display.

"Yes, young man," he said. "U.S. Eighth Army, the Battle of Mindanao."

Sam looked at Dad. It was weird to hear him referred to as a young man but compared to Mr. Merton he was young!

"Our Uncle Tom has received a Purple Heart," Sam blurted. "He was in Afghanistan and so is Uncle Alex. And Dad," Sam paused and reached over and grabbed Dad's hand, "he was in the Air Force."

"Well, well," Mr. Merton said. "A military family. That is a lot to be proud of."

"Madison's dad, the "Uncle Tom" Sam mentioned," Dad said aloud, "was wounded in the recent conflicts in Afghanistan." He turned to Madison but she was staring at the floor.

"I am sorry," Mr. Merton said to Madison. "Terrible, just terrible." He paused for a moment. "Back when I fought, we thought we were fighting the war to end all wars. Sorry the young men and women have to be involved these days. Hard thing, hard thing."

"Is this from Japan?" John asked.

"Yes, young man," he answered. "We were involved in the occupation, too. Beautiful country, Japan."

John was looking at faded hand-painted postcards of cherry trees and Buddhist shrines. There was also a Japanese sword. Madison came and stood next to him and she picked up a tiny Japanese doll dressed in a miniature kimono with small wooden sandals on its white cotton feet. It had a porcelain head with painted black hair and rosy cheeks and a tiny mouth.

"Be careful with that, please," the old man said. "That was something I sent to my little girl when I was over there. Sentimental value to me."

"Yeah, Madison," Brian said.

"You can mind your own business..." Madison said but was interrupted by Aunt Leanne.

"Come on, you two," she said and nudged Madison who replaced the doll, shrugged, and walked away. Aunt Leanne looked to Mr. Merton, "her dad sent her a small doll from Afghanistan before he was hurt."

Mr. Merton turned his eyes toward the floor, "I understand."

"Look," Sam said. She pointed to a scroll that had a painted koi fish on it. There was writing in Japanese characters in the lower right hand corner. The flowing fins of the fish were beautiful painted on a blue background. "It's a symbol of presever..." Sam stumbled on the word. "Per..."

"Perseverance," Mr. Merton laughed again. "My! You are a knowledgeable group."

"What's that mean?" Brian asked.

"Hmm," the old man thought for a moment. "Just the courage to hang in there, I guess you could say. You folks staying through the weekend?" Mr. Merton asked.

"Yes," Sam answered.

"Well, you should come to downtown Coupeville for the Memorial Day parade on Monday. Starts at 11:00 a.m. You kids especially. We could use some more flag wavers in the parade. Just show up down at the rec hall on Main Street and pick up a flag. Can't miss it, there's only one street in town."

"Can we, Dad?" John asked, "that would be so cool."

"Me, too?" Brian looked at his mom.

"Sounds like fun," said Aunt Leanne looking around at Mom and the others. She moved next to Madison and put her arm around her shoulder. "Your dad would've enjoyed this." Aunt Leanne squeezed her daughter's shoulder and for a moment, Madison laid her head on her mom's shoulder.

"He's supposed to be here," Madison said.

"I know, honey. I know."

"Your dad was wounded? He still over there?" Mr. Merton asked and looked up at Madison.

"No. He's been in a VA hospital," she answered. "He was supposed to be home this week."

"You know it's hard for dads to be away from their families. My daughter was your age when I was in the war. I sent her this little doll from Japan."

Mr. Merton reached over to the tiny doll in the kimono with his trembling hand and gently patted the doll on the table.

"It's not like soldiers choose one thing over another," he said. He looked up at Madison. "I like to think it was all about the same thing, the things we love. It's a hard thing to explain. Her dad knows what I am talking about." Mr. Merton nodded his head toward Dad and Sam grabbed his hand.

"Well, if you'll excuse me," Mr. Merton said. "I need to take a quick break." He stood up with difficulty. "You go on and enjoy the rest of the exhibit. And get outside on this beautiful day." He stood up slowly a little stiff. He reached across the card table found the edge of the tablecloth and laid it carefully over his collection. "You folks have a good day, now." He raised his hand in a wave and hobbled away.

"Thanks Mr. Merton, see you later," John called after him.

The family wound their way through the rest of the exhibit and at the end, Sam held open the big glass-and-wrought-iron exit door. Outside in the bright, noonday sun, everyone talked excitedly about the exhibit and John expounded on more details of the fort.

Sam wished she had brought her journal. She would love to sit down right now on the big stone steps of the lighthouse museum and write about the things she had seen.

The events of the last two days seemed oddly connected. Kacey Farmer and Madison, koi fish tattoos and Japanese scrolls, medals and the word valor. It felt jumbled inside of her and this was a time when writing in her journal helped her make sense of her feelings.

"How about lunch?" Mom asked everyone.

"For sure, let's head home," Jenny said. She went over and untied Chestnut from the bike rack where Mom had left her and the big dog gave her hand a sloppy kiss.

"Where's Madison?" Sam asked.

"She probably ran ahead," Brian said. "Good riddance."

"Brian," Aunt Leanne said.

The family walked across the parking lot but Sam went back to the big door. The door window was covered with black metal mesh and she held her hand over her eyes and pressed her face against it to see inside. The people on the inside looked blurry and squiggly but she spotted Madison back at Mr. Merton's table. Mr. Merton was still gone and in a split second, Sam watched Madison reach under the tablecloth and quickly put something in her pocket.

Sam stepped away from the door and leaned against the wall of the lighthouse just as Madison burst out of the door.

"Where were you?" Sam blurted.

"What?" Sam had startled Madison but she quickly caught herself. "I was just tying my shoe. Where is everybody?"

Sam pointed across the parking lot.

"Headed home."

"Well, let's go!"

CHAPTER 6

In Search of Pie

Sam stood on the lighthouse steps and watched Madison run to catch up with the others.

She acted as if nothing has happened, Sam thought. Suddenly, she was filled with doubt. What had she seen? Did Madison really steal something from the friendly, old man?

In the distance, her family looked so happy right now. Dad and Uncle Bruce were passing the football and John and Brian were tearing handfuls of grass and throwing them at each other and yelling. As usual, Jenny had her headphones on and followed Chestnut who had her nose to the ground. Madison ran up alongside Aunt Leanne and Mom and walked along as if everything was fine.

What about Mr. Merton's happiness? Sam thought. *What about his medals and artifacts that mean so much to him?*

Sam wasn't sure what to do. If she told Mom and Aunt Leanne about her suspicions it might be just like the scene at breakfast and nothing would change. Madison would be rude and deny everything and her mom would back off. If she told Jenny, well Jenny wouldn't be surprised at their "ballistic" cousin but it would make her even more mad at Madison. Sam remembered how John and Brian had chosen not to react when Madison locked them in the dungeon.

That would be her strategy for now.

I'm not going to ruin this perfect day with a scene, Sam thought. She ran down the museum steps to catch up with the group just in time to hear John complain.

"I'm starved!" John yelled.

"You're always starved," Sam said.

Madison looked over her shoulder at Sam but Sam ignored her. A football flew overhead and distracted her from her worry as Dad ran by and made the catch.

"Honey!" Mom yelled after him. "He's a lunatic with that football," she said to Aunt Leanne.

"You're lucky he can run around," Aunt Leanne said.

"Oh, Leanne, I'm sorry," Mom said and put her arm around her shoulder. "I wasn't thinking of Tom."

"It's okay," Leanne said. "I just hope they can fix his leg."

"They do amazing things with surgery and physical therapy these days," Mom said.

Sam listened to the conversation and watched Madison out of the corner of her eye. Mom knew what she was talking about. Dad was a surgeon and he knew all there was to know about the miracles that were being performed on the battlefield and in the operating room. Sam felt a surge of pride for her dad and her family.

"Hey, John," Sam asked. "Where's your backpack?"

"Oh my gosh," Brian said to John. He dropped the fistful of grass he had in his hand. "You left your gear at the museum."

"Oh, man!" John said. "Mom?"

"You two just run back," she said. "We'll have lunch figured out when you get back."

"Let's go," Brian shouted. The two boys raced off.

"I heard there's a tavern nearby that's famous for fish and chips," Uncle Bruce said. He ran by Mom and Aunt Leanne and threw a pass to Dad. "How about the grown-ups going to town?"

"What about the kids?" Leanne asked.

"We're not kids!" Madison said.

"We can handle it," Sam said. "There is plenty of sandwich stuff!"

"Sounds great!" Mom said.

They reached the house and Sam sat down on the lawn. Patches of tiny white daisies grew in clumps in the green grass and she began to pick them.

"Great, we're left with the troublemaker," Jenny said to Sam as she sat down next to her in the grass. "What are ya doin'?"

"Trying to make daisy chains," Sam said.

"Show me," Jenny said.

Sam and her buddies Sonja and Abby had learned to make daisy chains at recess in the fifth grade. She and her best friends had been in the same class that year and it had been the best year ever.

"Pick the daisy so that it has a long stem," Sam said. She reached into the grass and pulled at a flower. "It won't work if the stem is too short." She held one up for Jenny to see. "Then you put a tiny slit in it with your fingernail."

This part of making the chains was hard for Sam. Anything that took fine motor things, tiny movements and measurements, challenged her. But Sam loved challenges. She showed Jenny and then picked up another daisy and put its stem through the narrow cut in the stem.

"Then you slit the next stem and keep attaching them. You can make a necklace or a crown."

"Hey, you're doing a good job! This isn't easy," Jenny said. "Been a while since I've done this. How about you find the right flowers and I'll make the little cuts in the stem."

Sam gave her sister a big grin. Jenny was the best sister in the universe. It was so fun to sit and do something low-key and easy. Sam wondered if all the fun stuff went away when you got older. She thought for a moment about Mom and Aunt Leanne's conversation and all the responsibilities of being an adult. Sam wanted to be older and be responsible, too, but right now being a kid felt good.

"Jenny, I think I saw…" Sam said. She put her hand on Jenny's arm but she was interrupted. Madison sat down next to them on the grass.

"What's up?" Madison asked.

Jenny ignored her and turned to Sam, "What were you going to say?"

"Nothing," Sam said.

Jenny shrugged and gave Madison a look and then slipped her earphones back on and kept attaching the daisies. Sam felt the special moment with her sister disappear with Madison's arrival.

"We're making daisy chains," Sam said.

"What's her problem?" Madison asked. Sam shrugged.

Sam watched Madison pick a flower and when she tried to follow Sam's example, the stem broke.

"The stem was too short," Sam said.

Madison tossed the flowers over her shoulder and turned away from Sam and stretched out on the grass and closed her eyes.

Sam looked at her. Even with eyes closed, Madison had an expression on her face that Sam had seen before. Yesterday, when Kacey Farmer had been escorted out of the gym she'd had the same look on her face, the look that said, 'I don't care. I don't care about anything.'

Sam felt a wave of courage. She should do it right now! She should confront her right this minute! Madison with her bright red bangs and Kacey with her fish tattoo, maybe it was just like Brian had said, ways of getting attention. Sam finished the chain and looped the two ends together and held up the circle of flowers to admire.

"That's pretty," Aunt Leanne said. She came down the steps of the house and sat down. Madison heard the comment and sat up. She looked at the flowers.

"Cool," she said.

"Here," Sam held the chain out to Madison. "I can make another one." Sam felt discouraged that another moment had come and gone to talk to Madison. She let it go, for now.

"How do I look, Mom?" Madison asked as she put the crown on her head.

"Very nice, Maddie," Aunt Leanne said. "Here come the boys."

Sam and Madison looked across the field. John and Brian each held on to a strap of John's backpack and they were running.

"Will you please keep an eye on Brian while we go eat? It won't be more than a couple of hours," Aunt Leanne asked.

"I guess," Madison said. She was gently feeling the flowers on her head.

"There's some brownie mix in the kitchen. Maybe you could make some brownies for dessert tonight?" Aunt Leanne said. She turned to Sam. "She loves to bake."

"I'd rather make a pie," Madison said.

"You can make a pie?" Sam said in surprise.

"She's the queen of pie baking," Aunt Leanne said. "Our neighbor taught her."

"My dad would be blown away if you made a pie, oh my gosh, you have no idea!"

Aunt Leanne reached into her purse and pulled out her wallet. She handed Madison a ten-dollar bill.

"I think there is sugar and salt in the kitchen but you'll need flour and shortening," she said.

"I know, I know," Madison said as she took the money.

"There's a little store down the road a ways," Aunt Leanne said. "Maybe Jenny can drive?"

"Drive where?" Dad said as he came out the screened door. Uncle Bruce and Mom were right behind him.

"Madison's going to bake a pie for dessert and she needs to get to the store."

"A pie?" Dad asked. Sam watched as he lit up like a little kid at Christmas. For a moment, she felt a flash of jealousy. "What kind of pie?" They all looked at Madison.

"Hmm, this time of year? Cherry or apple, probably."

"I haven't had a cherry pie in forever," Dad said.

"That is my dad's favorite," Madison said. "Okay, cherry pie. Can we take the car?"

"You can walk," Aunt Leanne said. "And take the boys with you."

"And the dog. You can all go on a little walk," Dad spoke loudly and gave Jenny a nudge on the shoulder. She dropped an earphone and looked up at him from her daisy chain. "Everybody on a little walk to the store after lunch? You're in charge?"

"Sure," Jenny said.

"Dad! Dad!" John yelled.

The boys reached the front porch and dropped the backpack and collapsed on the grass gasping.

"You'll never guess!" John said.

"What?" Mom asked. Jenny took off her headphones and the boys had everyone's attention except for Madison who turned away from the boys as they approached.

"The police!" Brian said. "There were two police cars there with their lights on parked right in front of the museum."

"The police?" Sam asked and with a sinking heart she had a feeling she knew why.

"I was a suspect!" John said this mysteriously with pride in his voice.

"A suspect?" Dad asked.

"Yeah, there was a robbery."

"But we were just there. What was stolen?" Dad asked.

"Old Mr. Merton. Somebody stole his Medal of Honor. Can you believe that? Stealing a Medal of Honor? That's like the total opposite of honor."

"Oh, no," Mom said. "The poor guy. How awful.."

John was right, Sam thought. Stealing was certainly the opposite of honor. She stared at the bunch of tiny daisies she had picked and took a sidelong glance at Madison who was holding completely still. Sam knew she was listening to every word.

"That is a cowardly thing to do, for sure," Uncle Bruce said. "Did you see Mr. Merton?"

"Yeah," Brian said. "He was so upset they had to call his daughter to come and pick him up. I felt so sorry for him."

"I hope we still see him Monday at the parade," John said.

"Well, the police will get to the bottom of it. They usually do," Dad said. "People who do stuff like this get their punishment."

"Adam Sizer got expelled from school for theft," Jenny said. "It went on his permanent record."

Madison sat down now. She nervously picked some daisies and twirled them in her hand.

"Why didn't he go to jail?" John asked.

"He was under eighteen. But he had to spend a month in juvenile detention and do community service," Jenny said.

"People don't care what kids do," Madison blurted. "It's not that big a deal."

"Really?" Jenny asked. Sam's heart sank as she watched her sister turn to Madison. "People do care, people that aren't like you. People have respect for others' feelings and their stuff."

"Jenny," Mom said. She stepped over to Jenny and Madison.

"What?" Jenny said. "She knows the difference between right and wrong but she doesn't follow any rules."

"Jenny!"

"You haven't been with her all morning," Jenny continued. "Everywhere we've gone this morning, she has been a total pain. Ask Brian and John. Everybody is doing their best to get along and she is always doing exactly the opposite!"

Sam's heart was pounding.

"She locked us in the dungeon at the fort this morning," Brian chimed in.

"That was just a joke," Madison said. She turned to her mother. "Really, Mom, I wouldn't hurt these guys."

"Yeah, right. You probably stole the medal. Mr. Merton told you to leave his stuff alone. It would do you good to get punished for a change!"

"Now, that's enough, Brian," Aunt Leanne said. "Maddie was with us at the museum. That's impossible."

Sam's heart sank. She knew the truth and she couldn't say it. *What was wrong with her? What kind of punishment would Madison get expelled like the boy Jenny talked about?* Sam wondered.

"Well," Dad said, "we will probably get the details on Monday if we see Mr. Merton at the parade."

"I wish there was some way I could help him," John said.

"You guys leave the policing to the police. They know what to do." Uncle Bruce said.

The grown-ups loaded into Uncle Bruce's car and Sam caught Madison nervously chewing her bottom lip. The car pulled out and Bruce honked and waved as they drove down the driveway.

"I'm hungry!" John said.

"You're always hungry," Sam said.

They all straggled inside and it didn't take long to eat a quick lunch. Madison found a pie plate and a rolling pin in the back of a cupboard and Sam watched while she wrote her grocery list on her hand in pen. Jenny bossed the boys around and made them clean up and soon they were on their walk to the store but not before Sam ran upstairs and grabbed her journal.

"What's that?" Madison asked.

"My journal." Sam held up the book. It was almost full; the pages bulged and the cover was bent at the edges. "I write and draw stuff." Sam wanted to tell Madison that the journal was the place that she worked out all of her weird feelings, anything that bothered or confused her or made her unhappy, rather than stealing things. But she didn't.

"What kind of stuff?"

"Everything!" John said as he and Brian kicked rocks down the driveway.

"Let me see!" Madison said.

Sam opened her journal to the picture of the koi fish with its flowing fins and tail. The orange and black drawing seemed to swim off the page.

"Wow!" Madison said. "Wish I could draw!"

"You could if you wanted to," Sam said and closed the journal. "Everybody can draw. At least, that's what my art teacher tells us."

"I don't know about that," Madison said and kicked a rock across the road.

There were very few cars on the road and on each side there were deep ditches. Newly plowed fields the color of coffee grounds made a crazy curved pattern. In the distance Sam could see a huge tractor in a cloud of dust slowly plowing the huge field. Across the road, a herd of black and white cows nibbled the short green grass.

The little store was a low building with a fake country-style wooden porch. Inside the front door, there were two game machines and John and Brian ran over and pretended to work the controls.

"Jenny...?" John started to ask.

"No way," she answered and leaned against the wall by the doorway. The boys turned back to their pretend game and made exploding and shooting sounds.

"I'll be right back," Madison said.

"Can I buy us some Red Vines?" Sam asked her sister. Jenny reached into her pocket and pulled out five dollars and handed them to Sam. She grabbed a pack of the red licorice and stood behind Madison in line. "Did you find everything?"

"Think so," Madison said. "I have to use canned cherries but that's okay and I got some ice cream."

"We'll have to hurry back," Sam said.

The girls headed out and Jenny followed. The boys were lost in their pretend video games but Sam knew how to get their attention.

"Red Vines," she yelled and waved the package in the air.

Everyone helped themselves to the candy and they wandered back toward the house in the sunshine. John and Brian jumped across the ditch and walked along the barbed wire fence.

"Hey, you two! Get back over here!" Jenny yelled.

Brian and John ignored her and started mooing at the cows. Sam watched as the big animals simultaneously lifted their huge heads and looked at the two boys. The cows kept on chewing and the boys kept on mooing.

Madison stopped and without saying anything, she handed Sam the grocery bag and jumped across the ditch. To everyone's surprise, she quickly held two strands of barbed wire apart and climbed through the fence.

"Madison!" Brian yelled after his sister.

"Moo!" John continued yelling and Brian joined in.

One of the cows snorted but Madison kept walking toward the herd. John and Brian continued to moo and the big cow threw its head back and mooed back. John, Brian, Jenny, and Sam all laughed but stopped abruptly when the big cow started to walk toward Madison. The other cows followed the leader and then they began to trot.

"Get out!" Brian yelled.

Madison turned and ran. The cows followed, speeding up a little. Jenny and Sam clambered over the ditch and stood next to the boys and watched as Madison bent down to climb through the fence but stopped halfway through the barbed wire.

"Help!" she yelled. Sam saw that her hair was caught in the barbed wire. "Help!"

"I got it," John said.

Very quickly, the herd of cows had Madison cornered and the leader walked up to her and nudged her with its big head.

"Help me!"

John reached into his jeans and pulled out his pocketknife.

"Oh no," Madison yelled. "What are you going to do?"

As she spoke, the cow sniffed her. From where she stood, Sam could smell its grassy breath and see its long eyelashes and slimy nose. With a movement of its head, the big cow licked the side of Madison's face.

"Ahhh," Madison screamed. She tried to pull away but her hair was completely tangled in the wire. The cow sniffed her again and this time, it licked the daisy chain off Madison's head and chewed it.

Jenny started to laugh and Brian joined in.

"Madison got kissed by a cow! Madison got kissed by a cow!"

"Get me out of here!" Madison cried.

John acted quickly and with one slice of his pocket-knife, he cut off a chunk of Madison's hair and she climbed through the fence and stood up.

"Oh no, oh no!" she yelled. "Oh my hair!"

She groped the side of her head. John had made a mess of it. He'd managed to cut off a big piece of hair from the side of her face and a small chunk of red bangs. The hair hung on the barbed wire and moved in the slight breeze. Madison looked at it woefully while she held her hand to the side of her head.

"Madison got kissed by a cow!" Brian taunted. "Madison got kissed by a cow!"

Jenny kept laughing and Sam waited for Madison to go ballistic but instead Madison started to laugh.

"That cow had bad breath!" she said, laughing harder. "And its tongue was really rough!" She rubbed her cheek.

"Nice to know somebody loves ya!" Brian laughed.

"Even if it is just a cow!" John added.

"Does my hair look too terrible?" Madison asked as she turned to Sam and Jenny.

"Yeah, it's bad," Jenny said. "Kind of punk, maybe."

"Oh my gosh, the ice cream is melting," Madison said.

"Dad will be sorry if there's no ice cream," Sam said.

They jumped across the ditch to the road and Madison took the groceries from Sam.

"I'm not going to forget this weekend," Madison said. "Let's go make a pie for Memorial Day."

Sam and Jenny looked at each other and back at the strange girl with the weird hair.

"For our dads," Madison said.

Maybe Madison did care about something after all, Sam thought.

From Sam's Top Secret Journal:

I am pretty sure that Madison stole Mr. Merton's medal. I hate keeping this secret and I don't understand why I just don't go tell Mom. Something is holding me back, like another solution will show up if I am patient.

I asked Mom again if I could dye my hair. It's not like she can't see that EVERYBODY DOES IT! She says that I'm not Madison. I know that, I know that I am ME, but why can't I be like other people and do dumb stuff sometimes? Why is doing the right thing always the ONLY thing?

Anyway, I sure don't want to be like Madison. Her favorite thing seems to be being rude. But I like her hair. Really, her red bangs are about the coolest thing I have ever seen.

Although, her hair is a little messed up now after the cow incident.

After dinner, Uncle Bruce pulled out his guitar and played two songs and Madison sang with him. She has the prettiest voice. She changes when she sings, like it comes from the best part of her.

SHE SHOULD JUST SING ALL THE TIME!!!!!

Tomorrow afternoon, we're all going to town for ice cream. I think Jenny and I might go swimming at the pool in the morning. I have too many things on my mind; hope I can sleep!

CHAPTER 7

Kites, Swimming Pools, and Ice Cream

"Who wants to fly some kites?" Uncle Bruce stuck his head into the kitchen where the family was lingering over pancakes and bacon.

"Who has kites?" John asked.

"I do!" Uncle Bruce answered. "There is a great breeze right now!"

Dad jumped up.

"Great idea. Let's get these dishes done, boys," Dad said to Brian and John.

Jenny, Sam, and Madison took their plates to the sink and followed Uncle Bruce out into the yard. He had brought three kites. Two small, triangular ones with long, colorful plastic tails and one big kite made out of nylon fabric. It looked a lot like a parachute and it had two handles instead of one roll of string.

John and Brian burst out the front door.

"Whoa, cool," Brian said.

"I only brought three," Uncle Bruce said. "We'll have to take turns."

Jenny and Sam stood behind John.

"Please can we go first?" John turned and looked at his sisters. Sam wasn't too sure she could handle a kite on her own and she looked at her sister.

"We talked about going swimming," Sam said to Jenny.

"Yeah, we did," Jenny said. "Would you rather do that, Sam?"

"Perfect," John said. "You guys go swim and Brian and I will fly the kites with Uncle Bruce."

Uncle Bruce looked up at his nieces and smiled. Sam knew he was grateful he didn't have to choose who would go first.

"Hey, can I go swimming?"

Jenny and Sam turned to see Madison in a sloppy T-shirt and her pink, plaid flannel pajama bottoms. Brian looked at John and put his finger to his lips. John turned to the kites and pretended to fuss with something.

"Whatever," Jenny said.

Sam sighed. Another sister moment was going to bite the dust and she watched Brian happily give John a thumbs-up.

The girls grabbed their gear and Dad gave Jenny permission to drive the van to the pool.

Jenny brought the van to a stop in the gravel parking lot in front of a sign hanging lopsided on a wooden fence:

Fort Casey Pool; Open Memorial Day Weekend-August:
Daily 10:00 a.m.-5:00 p.m.
Admission: $2.75 ages 12 and up, $1.50 Kids under 12/
Seniors

"Bring your money," she said. "I'll lock the car."

Her words broke the silence of the ten-minute car ride. Sam knew that Jenny was still mad about yesterday with Madison and now she was even more irritated that she had to come with them to swim.

"Let's go," Jenny said.

Sam carried the plastic bag with her and Jenny's towels and swim gear but Madison brought her backpack with her. They paid at the counter, collected their locker keys, and went into the changing room.

Sam loved swimming and Jenny was on her school's swim team. Almost every Wednesday night, their family went swimming at the pool near their house in Seattle. The two sisters peeled off their jeans and sweatshirts down to their racing-style swimsuits and pulled their swim caps and goggles from the plastic bag.

Sam looked up to see Madison's feet sticking out from beneath a faded shower curtain hung across a changing booth then the curtain opened abruptly and Madison stepped out in a bikini that was a bright orange knit. It had strings that tied around her neck and her back and the front had a brass metal loop that gathered the fabric across the top in a flattering way. Her skin was stark white against the vivid color.

"Cute suit," Sam said.

Madison immediately hunched over and wrapped her towel around herself.

Sam felt confused. On one hand, she wondered if there was anything about Madison she didn't admire and on the other hand, Sam knew she was nothing but trouble. Madison reminded her of the skinny girls at school who didn't seem to care about anything and got all the attention. Sam felt like she cared too much and that she tried too hard.

"What? Are you two on the swim team?" Madison said. Sam wasn't sure if she was changing the subject or being sarcastic. Sam had a hard time understanding sarcasm.

"Jenny is," Sam said. "I'm more of a rock climber."

"Hmm," Madison said. "So, let's go swim."

They walked out into the noise and sunshine. Madison went to the edge of the pool and dropped her towel. She was painfully thin and Sam watched her hold her arms around her chest and jump straight in. She emerged gasping.

"Freezing!" she yelled.

Sam jumped in after her. The water was a little chilly but the warm sunshine and cold pool felt great.

"Want to go off the diving board?" Sam asked.

"No way," Madison said and started swimming to the ladder. She pulled herself out, her wet swimsuit hanging on her in a baggy way and she looked so skinny that, for a minute, Sam felt sorry for her. Madison picked up her towel, wrapped it around her shoulders, and sat over against the fence, her red bangs flattened down over her nose.

"You go dive, Sam," Jenny said. "Show her how it's done!"

Sam climbed out of the pool and walked confidently to the diving board. There was a short line, mostly high-school-aged boys who were jumping off the high dive and doing cannonballs. A group of girls were hanging on to the edge of the pool in the deep-end and they squealed at each splash that the boys made. One of the boys came up behind Sam and without pausing, stepped in front of her in line.

"Hey, no cutting," Sam said. He acted like he didn't hear her and Sam tapped him on the shoulder. The tall boy looked down at her. There was water dripping off his nose and his eyes were piercing blue.

"I was ahead of you," Sam said. Her words came out funny and she quickly looked down at the cement pool deck.

"Huh?"

Sam kept her eyes on the concrete but could feel him pause and look more closely at her. She knew the look. He was aware now that she looked a little different, that she was a little different. Sam said a quick prayer to herself, *please let him ignore me*. And the boy turned his back to her.

"Hey!"

An angry voice surprised Sam and a long skinny arm reached from behind her and tapped the boy on his shoulder again. It was Madison. She wasn't hunched but standing tall and her red bangs and black hair were pushed back from her face and her big eyes were beautiful. The boy turned, expecting to see Sam and was caught off guard by the force of Madison who looked like a character out of a graphic novel.

"Girls first!" Madison growled. She grabbed Sam's arm and pulled her in front of the tall boy.

"No way, now you're cutting!" The boy tried to be mad but Sam could tell that he was caught off guard by the tall, pale creature in the orange bikini. He went quiet and sulked.

Madison looped her arm through Sam's elbow.

"I can dive but not in this swimsuit! It would probably peel right off of me," Madison said. "You dive, I'll jump."

Sam laughed then stepped up the ladder and positioned herself on the low diving board. She remembered Dad's coaching and measured her three long steps to the end of the board, gave a jump and she was off. Sam cut through the water like a knife and came up for air in time to see Madison jump off of the high dive and land in a cannonball. She was so thin, she barely made a splash and she sunk deep into the water.

"Nice dive," she said to Sam when she came up. "I'm too cold. I'm going to go get dressed."

Madison dog-paddled away. Sam didn't even have a chance to thank her before Jenny swam up to her.

"Great dive, Sam," she said. "Let's go again."

The sisters took a few more dives and Sam excused herself to go use the restroom. She entered the locker room

walking carefully on the wet concrete and tile. A woman
sat on one of the low benches in the locker room and chat-
ted with a little girl while helping her get dressed. Sam saw
Madison's feet underneath the shower curtain again and
heard her softly singing one of Uncle Bruce's songs from
last night.

The shower curtain slid open and Madison stepped out
with her backpack over her shoulder and a big-toothed
comb in her hand. She saw Sam and moved to the counter in front of the mirror, threw down her backpack, and
started combing her bangs.

"How much longer you think we are going to be here?"
she asked.

"Not too long," Sam said. "Mom said to be back before
lunch."

"Oh yeah," Madison said. "So we can go get ice cream.
Whatever Mom says."

Sam loved ice cream but the way Madison said it, ice
cream sounded childish and silly. She went into the bathroom stall and Madison kept talking to her.

"You think your sister could stop at the grocery store?"
she asked.

"You can ask," Sam yelled through the door. She came
out and washed her hands in the basin next to Madison.

Madison leaned over the worn Formica counter and
peered at herself in the cracked mirror. She carefully part-
ed her hair above her bangs and pulled down all the pieces
of dyed hair. Sam watched in fascination.

"I need to touch up my roots," Madison said. She
stepped back and chewed her lip as she finished combing
out her long black hair. "You ever thought about putting
some color in your hair?" Madison ducked in to use the
bathroom before Sam could answer. "I could do it for you.
It's easy and only takes a couple minutes," Madison said
through the stall door.

Sam stood at the counter, shaking the water off her hands and wondering how to answer Madison. She would love to color her hair. Madison's backpack was open and Sam could see her wet towel wrapped around the orange swimsuit and its skinny straps hanging out. The front pocket was also unzipped and gaping open. It was stuffed with make-up and hair ties and ... Sam froze in shock. The toilet flushed behind her and Madison breezed out, still talking.

"Will you ask her for me?" Madison asked. Sam barely heard Madison's words. "Hey, anybody home in there?" Madison waved her comb in front of Sam's face and turned back to the mirror and gave her bangs another comb. "Will you ask her about the grocery store?"

"Okay," Sam said.

Madison jammed the comb into her backpack and zipped everything up and Sam pulled herself together and walked quickly away out the door to the pool.

"I'm waiting outside by the car," Madison called after her.

Sam spotted Jenny in the shallow-end talking to one of the high-school boys. Their eyes met and Jenny waved at her but Sam ignored her sister and walked the opposite direction to the line for the diving board. When it was Sam's turn, she chose the high dive this time.

She walked out to the end of the board. Sam wasn't afraid of heights. From where she stood, she could see Madison sitting on the curb next to the van combing her hair while she looked in a small mirror.

Had Sam seen what she thought she had seen? Mr. Merton's Medal of Honor jammed in to Madison's backpack. Her cousin had just helped her out with the boy who had cut her in line. She had done something nice for her. But now, Sam knew for sure that Madison had done something terrible.

Sam jumped off and held her knees tightly to her chest. For the seconds that she was falling, she forgot Madison, her red bangs and only felt the rush of air. The hard slap of the cold water and the silence of the deep waters came next. But when Sam came up for air, the confusion she felt was still there.

"You ready to go?" asked Jenny.

"Yeah," Sam said.

Sam took a deep breath and swam underwater to the ladder. She was afraid to look her sister in the eye, afraid that Jenny would see inside her head and know what she knew.

"Where's Madison?" Jenny asked.

"Out in the parking lot," Sam said. She hurried to the plastic bag hanging on a hook and grabbed her towel and clothes and disappeared into a dressing room.

"Madison wants to know if you will stop off at the grocery store," she yelled through the shower curtain.

"What for?"

"I don't know."

Sam was grateful she couldn't see Jenny.

"Sure, I guess."

The girls dressed and loaded into the car and drove the short distance to the grocery store. Jenny turned off the van and slipped on her headphones.

"I'll wait here," she said. She laid her head back and shut her eyes.

Madison hurried in, her backpack slung over her shoulder and Sam followed her. She stopped at a rack of postcards near the front of the store.

"Hey, it's the lighthouse. You should get some to show your friends." Madison pulled a postcard from the rack and handed it to Sam. "I'll be right back."

It was a picture of the Olympic Mountains and the beautiful view from Fort Casey. Night before last, Sam had enjoyed that view with her family but now she couldn't even focus on the picture.

Sam put the postcard back. She would see her best friends day after tomorrow; she didn't need to send them postcards. She walked toward the grocery aisles and looked at the overhead signs trying to decide which aisle would have the hair color for Madison.

"Let's go," Madison said.

Sam jumped. Madison had appeared behind her out of nowhere.

"But I thought you were getting…" Sam said.

"Just go," Madison whispered.

They walked quickly to the car and Sam climbed in after her. Jenny pulled one side of her headphones from her ear as she started the car.

"Did you get what you wanted?" Jenny asked.

"No. Couldn't find it," Madison said.

Jenny backed out and waited for traffic and pulled out onto the street then she slipped the one side of her headphone back over her ear. Sam knew that Dad told her not to drive and listen to her tunes at the same time. Madison stared intently out the window, her backpack clutched on her lap.

Sam buckled her seat belt and looked at the two older girls. As soon as they got back, she was going to grab her journal. She wished she had it with her now so that she could write down what had happened and try to sort it all out.

But for the time being, she felt crazy.

CHAPTER 7

Ice Cream and Red Hair

"How was the swim?" Aunt Leanne asked.
Everyone but John and Brian gathered around the table eating lunch. Madison didn't answer her mom but walked straight through the kitchen back to her room and slammed the door. The grown-ups were gathered around the table making sandwiches from bread, cheeses, and meats set out on the table.

"The water was a little cold," Jenny answered. "Where are Brian and John?"

"Those boys are crazy about that fort. We said they could hang out in the park and Uncle Bruce would meet them there after lunch. He didn't see it yesterday," Mom said.

"Do we have any peanut butter and jam?" Sam asked.

"What about going for ice cream?" Jenny asked.

"In a couple hours," Dad said. "Mom wants to kick back."

"In the refrigerator, Sam," Mom said.

Madison breezed through the kitchen.

"Where are you going, honey?" Aunt Leanne asked.

The slam of the front door was her answer. Sam grabbed two slices of bread from the table and made a hasty sandwich. Without saying anything, she left the kitchen and hurried upstairs to her room. Shutting the door behind her, she knelt on her bed and looked out the window. Madison was striding across the field.

She plopped down on the bed, took a bite of her sandwich, and chewed slowly. Her mind was whirling with the events of the morning. Madison! She was so crazy! Everything she did or said seemed wrong to Sam.

Sam couldn't think of a time that she had ever acted like that. Well maybe, a few times when she was mean to John but even that was more like being impatient. But being mean and breaking rules? Sam had to think. What had she really seen in the locker room?

Mr. Merton's Medal of Honor.

Sam pulled out her journal from under her pillow and opened it and grabbed a pencil. She focused on what she remembered of the medal and Mr. Merton's collection on the card table. Sam drew a square and sketched the items she could remember: the scrolls with the koi fish, the little Japanese doll, the postcards, and big sword plus army caps, button, and pins. She got her colored pencils out of her backpack and sat back down to color what she remembered of the medal. It hung from a beautiful blue ribbon that had tiny white stars on parts of it. The ribbon was braided and the medal hung with starry points and the word valor engraved at the top.

Sam admired her picture. Yes, this was what she had seen in the backpack.

She knelt up on the bed again. Madison was nowhere to be seen and Sam pictured in her mind the thin girl striding across the field. Had she walked across the field with her backpack?

Sam hurried out of the room and went downstairs. Uncle Bruce was in the hallway.

"Hey, Sam." He gave her a big grin. "I'm gonna go catch up with the boys. You can come if you want."

"Thanks," she said. Sam fumbled for an excuse. "I want to finish lunch."

"Bruce, keep an eye out for Madison. Maybe she went to meet the boys," Aunt Leanne called out. She, too, headed toward the front door. "I am going for a walk on the beach," Aunt Leanne said. "Anybody want to come along?"

"I'm sitting in that rocking chair on the porch and reading," Mom said. She gave Sam a quick hug as she passed her in the hallway. "What you up to?"

"Uh," Sam stuttered. "I was gonna see if there are any bananas left."

"On the counter," Mom said.

Dad was the only one left in the kitchen. He was finishing up the last of the dishes and wiping the counter down with a sponge. He reached into the trash can and cinched up a full garbage bag.

"Off to find the trash can," he said. He pulled Sam's ponytail and went down the back hallway toward the back door.

"Let me get the door," she said.

Sam followed him down the hallway past the bedrooms and opened the door and Dad lugged the garbage down the steps. She saw a dumpster down at the end of the driveway and realized she would only have a few minutes while Dad dumped the trash.

Sam stepped back in the house and hurried to Madison's room. It was a mess! The bed was unmade and a travel suitcase lay open on the floor with clothes spilled out all over the place. There was a small desk and chair in front of a window and on the chair was Madison's backpack. Sam went to it and unzipped the front pocket.

There was Mr. Merton's medal. Sam pulled it out and held it up and then quickly she stuffed it back in the pocket but not before she saw further into the pocket. It was a box of red hair color. The woman on the front had smooth long hair that was a brilliant color of red.

Sam thought back to the car ride and stop at the store. Madison said she didn't get was she was looking for. But here it was, the hair color. She was a shoplifter, too? The back door opened and shut and she held her breath. Dad! His footsteps became louder and then faded into the kitchen. She heard him call to Mom and then it was quiet. Sam stuck the box of hair color in the pocket and placed the medal back into the backpack as she had found it. She tiptoed over to the door and carefully listened through it, then opened it slowly and stuck her head out. The coast was clear.

She hurried into the kitchen, grabbed a banana, and hurried back up to her room. She sat down on her bed and pulled her knees up and hugged them. Sam was shocked at herself for being so sneaky but now she knew for absolute sure! Sam felt shocked at everything: Jenny driving with her headphones on, Madison, and the medal.

She picked up her journal and went downstairs to sit on the front porch. Mom was sitting in a big deck chair reading her book and she looked up at Sam and gave her a quick smile and disappeared into her reading. Sam sat down on a porch step, grateful that Mom didn't talk to her. Part of her wanted desperately to tell Mom everything but for some reason she couldn't, she just couldn't.

She opened her journal and saw her poem for the school assembly.

"With the things I like the best, I am always remembering."

She read the last line and was filled with sadness. Mr. Merton had lost a thing he liked the best. He had scolded Madison when she picked up the doll, told her that it had sentimental value to him. Did that make Madison mad? How could you steal from someone? Sam's thoughts poured out into her writing and she wrote and wrote and wrote.

"Hey, Madison," Mom said.

Sam shut her journal and looked up. Her insides jerked at the sight of her cousin and she felt anxious. Sam realized she had been fooling herself, trying not to create a fuss and believing the best of her cousin. Somehow, the truth had to come out but she still didn't see how.

Madison sat down on the step below Sam. She was a little out of breath. On the seat next to her, she lined up rocks she had collected on the beach. Sam noticed that they were all white.

"Those are pretty," Sam said. She didn't know why she said anything, she didn't even want to talk to Madison.

"I was looking at the rocks and suddenly all I could see were the white ones. They're great aren't they?" Madison said. She put them in different order and then shaped them into the shape of a small heart. "What are you doing?"

Without asking, she picked up Sam's journal and the book opened to the picture of Mr. Merton's collection.

"Nice," she said. She shut the journal quickly and handed it back to Sam. She looked out to the field where her mom, Uncle Bruce, and the boys were making their way back to the house. Brian began to run as they got closer to the house and Aunt Leanne was coming quickly after him. He stopped directly in front of Madison, his face red and angry.

"You," he yelled. "Why can't you just leave us alone? You have to do stuff to me on purpose! Why?"

Sam was sure he was going to hit her.

"Brian," Aunt Leanne said. "Stop now."

"Oh, right," Brian said. "Take her side! You always take her side and she just gets meaner. You don't know half the stuff she does. She locked us in a dungeon room yesterday and today, on purpose, she sneaks up on us and does it again."

"Madison," Aunt Leanne said, "what do you have to say for yourself?"

"I thought it was funny," Madison said. "They've got all these flashlights and stuff." She pointed at John's backpack. "It's not like anything would happen to them."

"That's not the point," Brian said. "I don't believe this. If Dad were here this wouldn't be happening."

"Well, Dad isn't here, is he?" Madison sneered.

"That's it, young lady," Aunt Leanne interrupted. "You're grounded for the afternoon!"

"Big deal, I'm gonna miss ice cream." And with that, she stood up and went into the house. The screened door slammed and then, the bedroom door slammed.

"I'm sorry, honey." Aunt Leanne reached to comfort Brian but he pulled away. She sat down on the step. "I'm sorry everyone."

"It's okay, it's okay. What about some ice cream?" Uncle Bruce said. "Maybe it's time to take that trip into town!"

Sam stood up and held her journal to her chest.

"I'm ready for ice cream!" she said.

"Here comes Jenny," Mom said. "Let's go!"

The family gathered and crammed into the van. Dad and Bruce sat up front and talked about football and everyone else gazed out the window. Sam felt happy to be leaving the house and Madison. It was a beautiful day and they were on vacation.

The little town of Coupeville was built on the edge of the saltwater. Mr. Merton was right, there only one main street in the town and it was decorated for the Memorial Day weekend. American flags lined the street and red-white-and-blue banners hung from most of the shop fronts.

On one side of Main Street, the businesses were mostly restaurants that took advantage of the beautiful view of the water. Signs advertising one version of, "View Dining at its Best" hung on nearly every one. On the uphill side of the street, old Victorian houses stood like gingerbread houses in their brightly-colored paint and window boxes. The houses were all shops now and had fun window displays.

"Hey, Mom," Sam said. "Bookstore!"

Sam and Mom loved bookstores. They both loved to read and Sam often found fun journals and cool pens and colored pencils. An old pier extended out over the water and a hand-painted sign said "ICE CREAM SHOPPE" in old-fashioned squiggly letters.

"Follow me!" Dad said.

The ice cream shop was crowded. Sam chose a waffle cone with two scoops of ice cream, one of coconut and one of chocolate. Everyone happily ate their ice cream cones and walked around the deck of the building.

Sailboats were tied up at the pier and they walked down the gangplank and past the beautiful boats. You could peek into the boats and see the small kitchen and seating areas. Sailing looked like fun to Sam although complicated. Out on deck, the different lines were carefully coiled and the big sails covered up under blue canvas. What would it be like to sail away to new places? Right now, Sam felt like she would be willing to go anywhere instead of back to the house and Madison. She took a big lick of ice cream.

"Look, the rec center," John said. John pointed up a side street. "Let's see if Mr. Merton is in there."

John took off with Brian close behind him. The rest followed, dawdling along and slurping and crunching the last delicious bites of their cones. As usual, Sam had ice cream all over her face and she paused to lick her fingers and wipe off the sticky mess.

Inside, they saw their old friend with other veterans who handed out furled flags. He was seated on a folding chair behind his card table of war memorabilia.

"Mr. Merton!"

John and Brian hurried up to him.

"You found it!" Mr. Merton laughed and his eyes disappeared into his wrinkly face.

"We hope we can help with the parade!" Brian said.

"You betcha," the old man replied. "You need to talk to these folks here. They'll set you up with flags for tomorrow."

John had paused over Mr. Merton's collection.

"We heard about the medal," John said.

"Well, you know, young fella," he paused, "it meant an awful lot to me, but it was just a thing. Things aren't the most important things in life."

"I'm still sorry someone was so disrespectful," John said.

Sam looked at the old man. He had a wistful look as he spoke and Sam felt a stab of guilt. She knew where the medal was and it wasn't this old man's fault. Her heart went out to him but somehow she couldn't speak. Would anyone believe her? Probably, but they would ask her why she didn't tell them right away. Sam knew she should've done that, and now, she felt guilty. She turned and walked out of the building.

Everyone came out in a few minutes carrying five rolled-up flags.

"Okay," John said. "Ten a.m. sharp tomorrow morning!"

"Yes sir!" Dad joked and saluted him.

Mom and Aunt Leanne wanted to get back to the house and get started on a big spaghetti dinner they had planned. Dad and Uncle Bruce had decided to go for a quick kayak paddle before dinner and they had promised a campfire on the beach after dinner. Aunt Leanne had brought graham crackers, chocolate bars, and marshmallows to make smores.

"But, Mom," Sam whined. "What about the book store?"

"Oh, honey, do I really need another book?" she asked.

"Yes you do, please," Sam said and grabbed her arm and pulled her a few doors down the sidewalk to the store. Aunt Leanne followed them.

Sam loved the smell of bookstores. They always smelled like paper and quiet. She wasn't sure how the peace and quiet could be part of a smell but it was. She walked over to a display of journals arranged in a basket.

A journal caught her eye that had Orca whales on the cover. There were also fun pens with cartoons of whales on them. Sam's whole family loved Orcas and every summer, they would be on the lookout for pods of whales as they rode the ferries up to their annual summer vacation in the San Juan Islands.

"Mom, look!" Sam grabbed a journal.

"Hmm, pretty cool." Mom walked over as though she knew the routine. Sam bought journals almost everywhere they visited. Mom was willing to buy them for her because Sam filled-up every single one of them with her writing and drawings.

Mom took the journal and turned it over and looked at the price tag.

"That's a good price!" she said. "Okay."

"And a new pen, please," she pleaded as she jumped up and down. Mom smiled at Sam and nodded.

"Anything for you, Leanne?" Mom asked.

"No, not today," she answered.

They met Dad and Uncle Bruce and the boys at the van. The boys were furling and unfurling the flags and waving them on the sidewalk.

"Don't let them touch the ground," Dad warned. "It's disrespectful. You'll have to be careful when you are walking in the parade tomorrow."

They put the flags away and Dad unlocked the van. Everyone piled in. Sam, John, and Brian jammed into the far back seat.

"I know where Mr. Merton's medal is," Brian said under his breath.

"What?" John asked.

"I'll bet you a million dollars that I know where Mr. Merton's medal is," he repeated. "Madison has it!"

"No way!" John whispered.

Sam held her breath and looked out the window. Brian was right and Sam knew it.

CHAPTER 8

Misunderstandings

Madison was sitting on the front porch combing her hair when the van drove up.

Sam picked up her journal and the bookstore bag that contained her new one and climbed out of the car and followed everyone up the front steps. She saw that Madison had dyed her bangs. Not only her bangs, but there was a brand new red stripe down one side of her long hair.

"You stole Mr. Merton's medal!" Brian stood defiantly in front of his sister.

"You're an idiot!" Madison said.

She stared her brother in the eye while she continued to run the comb repeatedly through her hair. Sam was mesmerized by the hair combing. The feeling reminded her of a movie she had seen in science class about cobras, their hypnotic gaze and deadly strike.

Brian stopped and faced the grown-ups.

"I know she did it," Brian said. "She was playing with stuff on Mr. Merton's table yesterday and Mr. Merton asked her to stop it." He turned to his sister again. "And you don't like anyone telling you what to do, do you Madison?"

"You don't know what you're talking about. Why me?" she said. "Why not her?" Madison pointed at Sam and then she stood up and grabbed Sam's journal and thumbed it open to the page of drawings. There, on the bottom of the page was Sam's sketch of the medal. "Seems like she is the one who liked the medal!"

The picture of Mr. Merton's medal was there for everyone to see. Sam stood with her mouth slightly open. She was frozen. She knew in her heart that she hadn't stolen the medal, but she didn't understand why she was keeping it a secret. Now she felt even more guilty, as guilty as if she had robbed Mr. Merton.

"Give her back her journal, Madison," Dad said.

Sam felt a huge sense of relief. He stepped forward and took the journal from Madison and gave it to her. He put his arm around Sam.

"I think everyone needs to calm down. Maybe you and Brian should apologize to each other and to Sam," he said.

"I still think you did it," Brian said.

"Brian!" Aunt Leanne said.

"Sorry," Brian said.

"Sorry," Madison said.

Sam heard the apologies but the words sounded hollow and angry. She knew it was a forced apology, the kind that you say but you don't mean.

"Come on, Brian," John said. He took his cousin's arm and led him up the steps.

"Well," Mom said, "dinner is in a couple of hours. Let's see if we can enjoy the rest of this Sunday afternoon. Our Memorial Day weekend is almost over."

As if on cue, Madison stood up and walked off. Jenny grabbed Chestnut and hooked her to the leash.

"I'm taking the dog on a walk."

The boys went into their room and Sam went to hers and sat on the bed. She wanted to do something but she didn't know what. The best thing would be to go straight downstairs and tell Mom what had happened but something was holding her back. Sam was positive that if she told a grown-up, they would just yell at Madison and it would be like everything that happened so far this weekend. Madison wouldn't care if she got caught or got grounded or that anyone was mad at her or that she had hurt anyone's feelings because Madison didn't care.

Sam tried to imagine what that felt like. It wasn't possible was it, to not care? She cared about everything: her family, Chestnut, her friends, school, her drawing, and writing. She cared very deeply about all these things. If you were a human being you had to care, deep down somewhere, you had to care!

Aunt Leanne said that Madison loved her father very much. Was it true? Were there people in the world who didn't love anything? Sam couldn't believe that.

"Hey, can we check something out your window?" John asked.

John and Brian were standing in her doorway. She could sense that they were up to something.

"Sure," she said.

They knelt on her bed and looked out the window.

"She's way across the field. Looks like she's headed for the fort," Brian said.

Both boys sprang off the bed and ran back to their room. With a sigh, Sam picked up her journal and stuffed her back pocket with colored pencils. She would go catch up with Jenny and Chestnut.

The holiday weekend had brought many families to the fort this afternoon. The air buzzed with shouts and laughter as kids and grown-ups played with kites, footballs, and soccer balls in the big field.

Sam spotted Jenny at the top of the trail to the beach. She started to run, her stride uneven and goofy. Sam's Down syndrome made it hard to run fast. That's why she loved rock-climbing. It was slow and steady and there was plenty of time to make decisions. Not like playing soccer where everything happened in a split second.

"Hey, squirt!" Jenny called to her.

Sam ran up to her a little out of breath.

"Come down to the beach with me," Jenny said. "If we go down far enough, we can let Chestnut off of the leash."

As if she understood every word, Chestnut looked up at Jenny and licked her hand. The girls laughed and started down the trail.

Although the sun was shining, across the big body of water the majestic Olympic Mountains rose above a layer of fog. Last week in art class, Sam had painted with Japanese sumi brushes and indigo ink. The ink was a deep navy-blue color and had a soft dreamy look to it. Sam thought that the mountains looked like sumi paintings today.

As the sisters walked on, the noise from the field faded away until there was only the sound of Sam and Jenny's steps on the crunchy sand and the soft riffle of the waves.

The bank above the beach where they walked became steep and a ways down it formed the sandy cliff that hid Fort Casey. Sam could see tiny figures of people standing at the fort on top of the cliff.

Jenny stopped and let Chestnut off the leash and she walked up from the water onto the driftwood.

"Let's build a driftwood house," she said.

Jenny grabbed the end of a long pole and wrestled it up over two huge stumps. She looked around for a similar pole and found it and dragged it and set it about three feet from the previous one.

"Now we can fill in the space with flat boards for a roof!"

Immediately, Sam was on the lookout for the right lengths of driftwood. They worked back and forth along the beach. Sam liked balancing on the logs and jumping from one to the other. In a short time, the two pole railings were covered with boards and their roof was complete.

Jenny wedged a long slender pole upright at the front of the driftwood house.

"Our flagpole!" she said.

Sam laughed and glanced around for something she might add to the house for decoration. She spotted it! There was a weather-beaten piece of plywood that had faint green lettering on it.

"...ISH"

Sam picked it up and carried it over to Jenny. Jenny had crawled inside the house and was smoothing a space to sit on the flat beach rocks.

"Look," Sam said as she held the sign up.

"I think it said '*FISH*'," Jenny guessed.

"Oh," Sam said. She was disappointed. "I thought it spelled '*WISH*'."

"Maybe it did," Jenny said. "I like '*WISH*' better anyway. Set it up outside here by the door."

Sam placed the square of wood near the door and then looked around for some small sticks. She found one with a fork in it and another small straight piece and she leaned them on the sign making a sort of '*W*'."

"Awesome," Jenny said. "Come on in!"

Sam crawled into the driftwood house and sat cross-legged next to Jenny. They sat in the shade with a few sun-beams shining through the spaces in the boards on the roof. There was a lovely view of the sparkling water and Sam felt safe and cozy.

"So, if this is our WISH house, we should each make a wish," Jenny said. "I'll go first. I wish that I see Gus again this summer at camp."

Gus was a boy Jenny had met last summer who she was secretly crazy about.

"Hmm," Sam thought out loud. She took a small stick and tapped Jenny on both shoulders. "Your wish is granted."

Sam paused. She knew what her wish was but she didn't know if she had the courage to ask for it. "I want to tell you a secret," Sam said. "And I wish that you won't get mad at me or tell Mom and Dad."

Jenny squinted into the distance and the sound of the water filled the silence. Jenny took the stick from Sam and tapped her shoulders, too. "Your wish is granted. So, what is it?"

"Okay." Sam took a deep breath. "Madison did take Mr. Merton's medal." Sam was silent then she added, "I snuck into her room after lunch and looked in her backpack. It's there. Please, don't be mad at me."

Jenny looked at Sam. "It's okay, Sam," Jenny said. "Tell me what happened."

The story poured out of Sam and Jenny nodded and listened patiently. When Sam was done talking, they sat for a while and gazed at the peaceful water.

"What do you want to do about it?" Jenny asked.

"I think I should tell Mom and Dad," Sam said.

"I agree but what would happen if we went to Madison and tried to talk to her first?" Jenny asked.

Sam's stomach jumped at the thought. "I don't know," she said. "Madison always gets out of everything. Do you think we could get her to give the medal back? Do you think she would ever apologize?"

"I don't know, but there is one way to find out. Maybe tonight after dinner, what do you think?"

"Okay," Sam said. "If you go with me."

They climbed out of the driftwood house and stood on a log and stretched.

"Chestnut!" Jenny called. "Where is that dog?"

"Down there!" Sam said. Chestnut was much farther down the beach and up at the base of the cliff and sniffing in the driftwood. "I hope she hasn't found something to roll in!"

"Chestnut!" Jenny called.

Chestnut didn't pay any attention to their calls and the sisters trudged down the beach until they reached her.

Sam looked up the cliff. She realized they were directly below Fort Casey. She could see heads of the tourists looking over the edge from the fort. At the bottom of the cliff was a sign that said, "NO ACCESS!" Sam saw the zig-zaggy trail that Madison had climbed yesterday.

She walked over to Chestnut who continued to sniff along the driftwood and at the base of the trail. The dog stopped and pawed the ground and Sam looked down.

A cell phone.

"Jenny!" Sam said. She bent over and picked up the phone. She turned it over and saw the name engraved on the back.

"What is it?" Jenny asked. She grabbed the dog and clicked on the leash.

"Madison's phone."

Jenny took it and looked at Sam.

"Maybe talking to Madison won't be so tricky after all!"

"Maybe not," Sam agreed. And when she said it, her stomach didn't jump.

From Sam's Top Secret Journal:

I am looking back at what I wrote on the porch today. The whole time I wrote I wanted so bad to tell Mom everything. But I didn't do it. I feel better after talking to Jenny at the beach. It was a relief.

Jenny and I have a plan. After the campfire tonight, we are going to try and get Madison to come with us to the driftwood house! Just so we can talk to her about the medal and maybe tempt her with her phone.

Wow! Is that blackmail?

Tomorrow is the parade and our last day at Fort Casey. We have to help Mr. Merton, we just have to.

CHAPTER 9

Beach Fires, S'mores, and Sunsets

D ad and Uncle Bruce were throwing the football in the big field when Sam and Jenny came up from the beach. Jenny thrust Chestnut's leash into Sam's hand and went running to join them.

"Dad," Jenny yelled.

Sam watched her sister run toward Uncle Bruce trying to intercept Dad's pass. Her uncle yelped with surprise as the strong girl sprinted in front of him and leapt up to snag the ball. Jenny fell to the ground and skidded on her shoulder before she jumped up with the football in one hand and did a victory dance!

"Touchdown!" Jenny yelled.

Dad and Uncle Bruce ran up to her and gave her high-fives while Jenny backed up running and prepared to launch another pass. Being Dad's oldest child, and being a girl, had given Jenny the dubious benefit of being raised something of a boy. Dad had been throwing the football for her since she was small and her natural ability was amazing. John would play sometimes, but he was more of a thinker and a designer than an athlete.

Sam was terrible at football but she could accept that; she knew she had her own talents. She held her journal close to her chest. Chestnut pulled on the leash and Sam decided to leave the sidelines and followed her.

Chestnut followed her nose and before Sam knew it, they had walked through the woods and were at the park by the fort. Sam stopped at a picnic table and looping Chestnut's leash around her foot, she sat down.

Sam started to draw the outline of the fort on the horizon. Even in the sunny afternoon, it had an ominous look. Sam liked drawing houses and buildings. Her art teacher, Ms. Sommers, had always told them to draw what they see not what they think they see. That was a hard idea for Sam but she practiced now, tracing the low outline of the fort and stopping and using her darkest colors to shade in the concrete doors and windows. She paused to admire her work. It was good!

She looked next at the green hillside and collected all of her green pencils. She was trying to decide which shade of green to start with when she spotted Brian and John in the distance. The two boys were down by a big rusty door on the fort and the far end of the building.

"Come on, girl," Sam said.

She closed her journal and jammed her pencils in her pocket and walked toward the boys.

"John!" she yelled.

From a distance, she saw her brother look up. He said something to Brian and in an instant they had grabbed their backpacks and took off. Chestnut gave a bark after them.

"Hey, wait up," Sam said.

Chestnut strained at her leash now pulling Sam across the grass to the concrete area where John and Brian had been. Sam's eyes followed the boys while the big dog whined and pulled at her. Chestnut sniffed at the bottom of a big rusty door and Sam saw that it was the same dungeon that John and Brian had been locked in yesterday.

Bang, bang!

Sam jumped back and Chestnut gave a short bark.

Bang, bang, bang!

Sam noticed that the chain was hooked again holding the door shut and she reached up and unhooked it and pulled hard on the broken door handle. The door creaked open and Madison burst out and ran across the concrete to the grass and sat down. She grabbed her knees and pulled them to her chest and rocked back and forth. Chestnut pulled free and bounded over and gave Madison a big, sloppy kiss.

To Sam's surprise, Madison burst into tears.

Chestnut looked up at Sam and cocked her head as if to say, what do I do now? She wagged her tail and whined. Sam wondered the same thing but she walked over and sat down next to Madison. She pulled out her green pencils, opened her journal, and continued with her sketch.

"What are you doing?" Madison asked. She gave a huge snotty sniff and wiped her nose with the back of her hand. Her red bangs were disheveled and her eyes were brilliant blue with tears.

"I'm drawing the fort," Sam said.

Sam held the drawing out for Madison to see. Madison tapped her finger on the big door in the drawing.

"That's where I was trapped!" She sniffed again. "I guess I deserved it after yesterday." Madison lay back on the grass, her skinny arms folded over her face. "How come you draw all the time?"

"It helps me with my thinking," Sam said. "I have to hold still to collect my thoughts sometimes; something like that. That's why I drew Mr. Merton's things."

Sam paused, hoping that Madison would pick up on the hint.

"I don't want to know my thoughts!" Madison said. Her voice sounded angry and sad at the same time. "I can't stand the things I am thinking."

"What do you mean?" Sam asked.

"I just make everybody mad anymore. It's like I can't help it. If someone is nice to me, or if I am nice to someone else, it's like I will start crying."

"What's wrong with crying?" Sam asked.

"It feels like if I start, I won't be able to stop."

"You just stopped," Sam said.

"I guess you're right," Madison said. She reached up and scratched Chestnut under her chin. "But I do bad things."

Sam kept on drawing. She hoped that Madison would confess to taking the medal and that she and Jenny wouldn't have to carry out their plan. Chestnut gave Madison another big lick.

"This dog is crazy!" Madison said. As if on cue, Chestnut started licking her face and her neck and stuck her nose in her hair. Madison laughed and rolled in the grass and hid her face. "Tell her to stop!"

"Chestnut!" Sam called. She reached over for the end of the leash and gave it a yank. "Come here, lie down now."

Madison sat up and looked at Sam's journal again.

"Is that where you write your poetry, too?" she asked.

"All the time."

"Read me something."

"Okay, here goes," Sam said. Sam turned back several pages to one of her poems. She took a deep breath and reminded herself not to rush so that each word would be clear.

Roots Before Branches

I pray that God will
Put dreams in your heart
My love gives you roots
I have tears as you take off
I'll cheer as you fly
Daring to do great things
We are one, we are a family.
May your passion be the wind
May your smile be the sun
As I see you smile it lights my day
When I see you laugh it fills my heart
All for one, in every seed there is a start
In every heart there is love because I love
you
You have the strength to carry on I know
it's hard
The right thing to do is to move on and have
faith

Don't let go of your friends keep them in
your heart
Believe in yourself it's the only way you
have a hero
In my heart I feel the sun blazing in my
heart I feel you
The light shows the way home the light
stays inside me
Your life is the branch, your love is the
root.

Sam finished and there was a long silence.

"That was kinda cool," Madison said.

"Thanks," Sam said, "Have you ever written poetry?"

"Well sure, in school," she said. "I've always wanted to write songs."

"Aren't songs poetry? You've got a great voice. You could write songs about all the stuff you don't want to think about."

"Yeah, but then I have to think about it!" Madison sighed.

"But you think about it in a different way. I think that's what artists do. I want to be an artist."

"How cool would that be?" Madison asked. "Hey, where'd the crazy dog go?"

The girls looked up and saw Chestnut walking toward a family spread out on the ground having a picnic.

"Whoa, we better grab her," Sam said. "Then we should probably get back."

"Okay," Madison said.

The girls went over and apologized to the people having the picnic for Chestnut who gazed hungrily at their sandwiches and walked back to the house.

John and Brian were waiting for them on the front porch steps and Sam wondered if Madison would explode. To her surprise and the boys' disappointment, Madison sat down on the stairs and petted Chestnut.

"Stay here," Sam said to Madison.

Sam ran in to the house and hurried up to her room. Jenny was laying on her bed with her bare feet up on the wall, listening to her music and didn't even notice Sam come in. Sam grabbed the bag from the bookstore and took out the new journal and pen and raced back downstairs.

Madison was still sitting on the steps with Chestnut and the boys had disappeared.

"Here," Sam said.

"What...?" Madison took the blank journal and the pen and carefully looked at it.

"Half the time I don't know what I'm gonna say," Sam said. "That's the cool thing about a journal, you don't have to *say* anything. You just start writing."

And with that, she pulled her pens and colored pencils out of her pocket and sat down next to her cousin. She placed the pencils between them on the step and went back to her drawing. Out of the corner of her eye, Sam saw Madison chewing on the end of a pen, lost in thought and staring out at the mountains and the water.

Then Madison bent down and started writing.

"John, you and Brian are in charge of the firewood," Dad said.

It was after dinner and they were getting ready to make the trek down the beach for a campfire.

"Can we build the fire, Dad? Please?" John begged and Brian looked pleadingly at Aunt Leanne.

"Absolutely, if you carry all the wood down to the beach! You might need to make two trips." Dad laughed and Aunt Leanne nodded.

"How about some marshmallow sticks, too?" John asked. Sam knew John was looking for an excuse to use his pocket-knife. "There are some small trees in the bushes out back. The branches would be perfect for roasting marshmallows."

"Great," Dad said. "But be careful!"

The boys took off to where the firewood was stacked behind the house.

"And here's some newspaper and a box of wooden matches," Mom called after them.

Mom brought the cooler with wheels into the kitchen and Sam helped her pack beverages and the makings for s'mores. Then they met the others on the front porch.

Aunt Leanne piled some blankets she had collected from the extra bedroom on top of the cooler and Uncle Bruce pushed through the screened door with his guitar.

"Can I carry that for you?" Madison asked.

"Can I carry something?" Sam chimed in.

"Sure," he said. "You can be my roadies."

He handed Madison the guitar case and gave Sam a music book titled, *Bruce Springsteen's Biggest Hits,* and they started down to the campfire.

Jenny followed a ways behind Sam and called to her.

"Sam," she whispered.

Uncle Bruce and Madison were talking about guitar chords and Sam fell back to walk with Jenny.

"Are you ready for this?" Jenny asked.

"I guess so," Sam said.

The sun was going down and the Olympic Mountains were pink and orange in the distance. Even thought it was almost summertime, the evening was cooling off quickly and a light wind came in off the water. Sam pulled up the hood on her sweatshirt.

"She's not a bad person," Sam said.

"How can you say that? She's crazy," Jenny said. "You're too nice to people, Sam. Some people just aren't nice."

Sam thought about this. She knew there were bad people in the world. She also knew the rules about not talking to strangers or walking alone at night and that kind of thing. But her cousin was different. Madison had a lot going on; she had told her so when they sat in the grass by the fort. If anything, Sam felt sorry for Madison and she was trying hard to understand her.

"Well, I thought if I was nice to her, she would tell me about the medal," Sam explained.

"She didn't, did she?"

"No," Sam confessed.

"See," Jenny said.

"So how will we get her to talk?" Sam asked.

"I think after we sit by the campfire for a while, we can tell her we want to show her our driftwood house," Jenny said. "And when we get in there, I'll confront her and show her that I have her phone."

Jenny patted the back pocket of her jeans where she had the cell phone.

"Okay, we'll do it your way," Sam said.

John and Brian had the fire started when they reached the beach. They had chosen a spot on the beach in the opposite direction of the "WISH" house and that worked out well for her and Jenny's plan.

"This is perfect!" Aunt Leanne exclaimed. "Tom would so love this."

"Maybe next year we could be here again," Dad said.

Jenny rolled her eyes at Sam but Sam liked the idea.

Sam chose a spot on a log near the fire but in a moment the smoke came in her direction and forced her to move.

"Smoke follows beauty," Mom said. "My grandma used to say that!"

Sam scooted over to where Aunt Leanne had spread a small tablecloth over a big log. The marshmallows, chocolate bars, and graham crackers were ready to go. Brian placed the cut-and-sharpened marshmallow sticks against the log. Sam took a stick and carefully put two marshmallows on the sharp end.

Sam had her own system for roasting marshmallows. She liked to cook them very slowly so that they were melted all the way through and had a golden brown crust on the outside. This took a lot of patience and she also had to be sure that the stick didn't catch on fire.

"A flaming torch!" John said.

John's approach was the exact opposite. He had stuck his marshmallow stick into the hottest part of the fire and now he waved the flaming marshmallow in the air. In a moment, he blew out the fire and slipped the charcoal outer coating off and stuffed it in his mouth. There was a smudge of charcoal on his chin.

"Perfect!" he said.

"What are we gonna sing?" Uncle Bruce asked. He reached behind the log and clicked open the locks on his guitar case. It was getting dark now and the guitar shined a golden red color in the firelight.

"Play that Springsteen tune that you and me and Alex used to sing," Dad said.

Mom and Sam and Jenny laughed at Dad. They had heard "Born to Run" many times. Dad had it on a CD in the van and sometimes they would be driving along and he would turn the volume up and sing at the top of his lungs. If you could call it singing.

Uncle Bruce began to strum. He started to sing and Madison joined in with her beautiful voice and even Sam's family seemed to handle the chorus. They all sang at the top of their lungs, "...and tramps like us...baby we were born to run."

The song ended and they all clapped. Dad leaned forward and put another log on the fire and the fire crackled and spit orange sparks into the night sky.

"Madison, come and sing something," Uncle Bruce said. "Let's do that song you did for school. I figured out the chords."

Madison was licking sticky marshmallow off of her fingers and didn't say anything for a moment.

"Come on," Uncle Bruce urged.

"Okay," Madison said. "This is from a solo I did for school choir last fall. It's called, 'We're Going to be Friends.'"

"I love that tune," Jenny blurted. "The White Stripes version."

Uncle Bruce started to play and Madison sang. Her voice was wistful and sweet and very beautiful. Sam could feel them all become captivated by the pale girl with the red bangs who sang so sincerely. The notes of the song were repetitious and the words repeated the wish to be friends.

Madison is a good person, Sam thought as she listened.

When the song was finished everyone applauded, even Brian and Jenny. Madison made a dramatic bow.

"I'll be signing autographs later," she said jokingly. She didn't sit down but climbed over the log and walked toward the water. Sam and Jenny looked at each other. The others had resumed talking and Brian and John were busy tending the fire. Jenny nodded to Sam and they slipped away after her.

After her eyes adjusted to the dusk, Sam could see Madison down the beach a ways. She was throwing rocks into the water close to the shore.

"Look," Madison said. "It's like a million little flashlights in the water."

"It's bioluminescence," Jenny said. "They are actually tiny creatures." She picked up a stick and splashed the saltwater. The bioluminescence lit up when the water moved and then faded away and Sam could see it in the waves as they broke gently on the sand.

"Cool," Sam said. "Hey, Madison, come see what Jenny and I built today."

"Where?" Madison asked.

Sam pointed up the beach and started walking. The flagpole was tilted slightly and Jenny repositioned it.

"WISH," Madison read Sam's sign. "This is cool."

"We made the 'W' and call it our WISH house," Sam said. "Come inside."

The three girls climbed through the opening and sat on the sand floor and looked out at the water. The night was dark but there were many stars in the sky and the air smelled salty and fresh.

Jenny reached into her pocket and held Madison's cell phone in front of her.

"Does this look familiar?" she asked.

"Oh my gosh, my phone!" Madison gasped.

She made a grab for it but Jenny pulled it back.

"We are going to do a little trade," Jenny said. "I have something that belongs to you and…" She paused and looked at Sam.

"You have something that belongs to Mr. Merton," Sam said finishing the sentence.

Madison sat up straighter and pulled her shoulders back and tossed her red bangs but then she sank back down over her crossed legs. She picked up a little stick and poked at the sand with it.

"You're right," she said. "I have it and I don't even know why I took it. I saw it and just got so mad about my dad. A stupid medal can't make up for someone's life. I know it's not the medal that has meaning; it's what people do. It's just my dad was hurt and I want him back." She dropped the little stick, put her hands together and asked, "do you really make wishes in this place?"

"Yes," Sam said.

"Well, I wish I had never done it," she said. "It's like sometimes I am just out of control. Help me. Help me figure out a way to give it back." She looked at Sam and then at Jenny. "Maybe we could just sneak over to the lighthouse and put it on the front door with a note or something."

Sam and Jenny just stared at her.

"If you did something that hurt someone," Sam said, "you have to apologize." Sam thought about Brian and Madison apologizing earlier today. "A real apology," she added.

"Tomorrow at the parade," Jenny said. "You can find Mr. Merton and give it back and tell him what happened."

"I can't," Madison said. "Everybody will know what I've done, I just can't."

There was the sound of footsteps outside the driftwood house and a flashlight shone in the door.

"Is that you, John?" Jenny said. "Go away."

Jenny quickly put the phone back in her jeans pocket as John and Brian crouched down in the doorway.

"Tomorrow at the parade," Brian said.

"You don't know what you are talking about!"

"Oh yeah?"

And with that, John reached in and held open the box with Mr. Merton's medal in it.

"You went into my backpack! You can't take stuff out of my backpack!" Madison said. She was outraged.

"Oh, right," Brian said. "I can't take stuff that's been stolen. You have to make this right, Madison, or I am gonna go over to the beach fire right now and show this to everybody."

As if to make his point, John shined the light in Madison's face.

"Turn that off, okay, okay," Madison said covering her eyes. "Give it back to me."

"No way," John said. "Jenny has your phone and we have the medal and you have to do the right thing tomorrow after the parade."

Sam, Jenny, Brian, and John waited.

"Alright. After the parade."

"Let's get back to the campfire," Jenny said. "And try and pretend none of this has ever happened."

From Sam's Top Secret Journal:

NEWS FLASH! Jenny and I (with the help of Brian and John) got Madison to agree to return the medal and talk to Mr. Merton tomorrow at the parade. She said she would. I have faith in her but Jenny doesn't.

My hair smells like a beach fire! We had an amazing campfire at the beach and roasted marshmallows and made s'mores. Uncle Bruce played his guitar and Madison sang. Even though she is hard to be around, she is very talented. I hope she writes some songs in her journal.

Tomorrow is the Memorial Day Parade and then we go home! Three-day weekends are too short but I'm done with all the Madison drama.

CHAPTER 10

Flags, Pride, and Honor

"John, grab the trash bag in the kitchen and take it to the dumpster!" Dad yelled.

It was a busy morning as everyone scurried around packing and cleaning up. The front hallway was stacked with duffle bags and coolers and other gear. It was Mom's idea to load up the cars and the van before the parade and then take off for the ferry ride home.

"This way we won't have to come home and make lunch and then clean up again," Mom said.

"I agree," Aunt Leanne said.

"We can have ice cream for lunch!" Sam said.

"Right," Mom said giving her a look.

Sam ran upstairs to her and Jenny's bedroom and knelt on the bed to take one more look out the window at the field, trees, and the trail to the beach. It was another sunny day and Sam wondered how long their WISH house would last down on the beach. Would other kids have fun playing in it, or would storms and waves sweep it away? Probably both.

Last night when she and Jenny and Madison sat inside and looked out on the reflection of the moon on the water, Sam had wished they could stay there forever. She thought about Madison's wish. Some wishes didn't come true. Maybe Jenny wouldn't see Gus again at camp. But Sam had her wish: she had told Jenny what Madison had done and asked for help. Her wish had come true.

When the cars were loaded up, the family gathered for a picture on the front steps of the house. Uncle Bruce stood in the middle between Madison and Sam with an arm around each girl's shoulder. Mom next to Sam and Leanne next to Madison filled out the row. John and Brian sat on the bottom step with John's backpack parked between them. Jenny sat with her arms around Chestnut.

"Hey, wait!" John jumped up and ran to the van and grabbed two of the rolled up flags. "Let's use these!"

"Keep them off the ground!" Dad reminded.

Brian and John unfurled the flags and the boys moved higher up the staircase and held the flags out to the side.

"Do we look patriotic?" Brian asked.

"It looks great!" Dad said. He held up his phone and snapped a picture.

"Let me take one with you in it," Uncle Bruce said.

He and Dad changed places and he snapped a few more pictures.

"Oh, Tom would've loved this," Aunt Leanne said. "At least, I can send him a photo."

"I wish he was here," Madison said.

"Yeah, but he's not," Brian said to her. "Why don't you just get over it? He's not here."

"Okay you two," Uncle Bruce said.

"Does everything have to be about her?" Brian asked.

Sam and Jenny looked at their cousin. After her promises from the evening before she seemed back to her old mean self. Sam knew that Jenny didn't have any faith in Madison but Sam was hopeful. Even though Madison had done a lot of dumb stuff this weekend, Sam liked her for some reason. She was willing to be different and Sam knew that being different wasn't all that easy.

They loaded up and Sam stared out the van window at the big house.

Goodbye old house, she thought. *Have fun with the next family.*

There was a lot of traffic as they approached the town of Coupeville and Dad slowed down looking for a parking place.

"Let's keep Chestnut in the car," Mom said. "Too many people."

They piled out and the five kids each grabbed a flag.

"Mr. Merton said to meet him in front of the rec hall," Brian yelled. The kids started walking down the block.

"We should go this way to find a good place to watch," Uncle Bruce said and he pointed in the opposite direction.

"Look for us along the way and wait at the end of the parade. We will meet you there," Dad added.

At that moment, Aunt Leanne's cell phone rang and her voice filled with excitement. "It's Tom. I need to take this," she said.

"I want to talk to him," Madison said.

"You have to go with the others," Aunt Leanne said. "You can call him later."

"Tell him I love him!" Madison yelled over her shoulder as she walked away with Sam and the others.

"Okay, Maddie," Aunt Leanne said and turned to walk slowly behind the other grown-ups.

Around the corner where the rec hall was located, the street was full of people preparing for the parade. Several men and women in uniform stood at the front of the parade and held a banner. Right behind them was a small marching band from the high school and then a small float.

"Sam!" Jenny called out. "Look at the banner!"

It took a moment for Sam to walk to the front of the crowd but then she saw the words on the banner.

"*Remembering,*" said the sign in huge red-white-and-blue letters. Underneath the word were the symbols of the different arms of the military.

"Wasn't that the name of your poem?" Madison asked.

"Yes," Sam said. She stood still, stunned.

"Freaky!" Madison said.

"Hey, it's Mr. Merton!" John yelled.

"Madison!" Brian was yelling at his sister and gesturing toward Mr. Merton.

Many of the veterans that had been at the lighthouse museum were seated on the float on folding lawn chairs along with Mr. Merton. The float was decorated with red-white-and-blue crepe paper and Sam grabbed Madison's elbow.

"It's your chance, Madison," Sam said. "Go talk to him."

Madison stood chewing her lip and started to walk toward him when a woman with a megaphone made an announcement.

"Everyone who is carrying a flag needs to line up right now in front of the Veterans' float," she said sternly. "I repeat, line up in front of the Veterans' float."

"Go!" Sam said.

Madison started over to Mr. Merton who saw her and Sam and waved at them both. Madison had almost reached him when the woman with the megaphone saw her and her flag and spoke to her. "ALL flag carriers report to the area in front of the Veterans float!" The woman said glaring at Madison. Madison turned and walked back to Sam.

"You promised, Madison," Sam said.

"I can't, this crazy lady is watching me!" Madison said.

"That's just an excuse," Sam blurted. "You did something wrong and you have to make it right!"

As Sam spoke, the woman with the megaphone interrupted her to announce the beginning of the parade. The band started to play loud and slightly out of tune. Sam and Madison stepped quickly back into position and held up their flags. The float with Mr. Merton gave a lurch and started to roll slowly down the street. Parade watchers were crowded along both sides of the street and as the band started to play, the crowd began to cheer.

Brian and John were enthusiastically waving their flags but Sam held hers listlessly. She felt confused and disappointed. Maybe there would still be a chance for Madison to do the right thing. The parade route was only two blocks long and it would be over very quickly.

Sam looked for Mom and Dad and the others but there were too many faces cheering from the sidewalk. Little kids were up on their parents' shoulders and people were taking pictures and waving and cheering while the band played "America the Beautiful." Beside her, Madison held her flag aimlessly and was hunched over and hiding behind her red bangs. They were almost to the end of the block when Sam spotted Dad and Uncle Bruce.

"Look!" Brian yelled. "It's Dad."

He thrust his flag into John's empty hand and pushed his way to the sidewalk and struggled through the crowd. Madison froze in her tracks and looked ahead. A tall man on crutch - his hair in a buzz cut and his skin as pale as a ghost- leaned against Aunt Leanne.

"Is it Uncle Tom?" Sam asked Jenny.

"I think so," she said.

It was Madison's turn to hand over her flag and push her way through the crowd.

"Dad," she cried. "Daddy!"

The parade moved to the end of the block and stopped. Police cars were parked at the end of the street, their lights flashing and blocking off the street. They were parked directly in front of Mom and Dad and the family. Sam's heart went to her throat. What if the police had figured out who the thief was? What if they were going to take Madison away?

Sam hurried to catch up with Brian and Madison. Everyone was hugging and crying.

"I can't believe it!" Madison said. "You made it, you made it." She leaned into her dad, her arm around his waist with his big arm over her shoulder.

"How are you, son?" Uncle Tom grabbed Brian with his other arm and gave him a bear hug and Brian beamed. "We're good, Dad. I mean, we're sure better now that you are here."

Sam walked up and whispered in Madison's ear and pointed to the police cars.

Madison's eyes grew big and she looked at Brian. He raised his eyebrows at her.

"Mr. Merton!" Madison yelled.

The Veterans' float had come to a stop nearby and the old men were being helped down from their seats. Madison tugged on her dad's hand.

"You have to come with me," she said to her dad.

"Now, Madison," Aunt Leanne said. "Take it easy on him."

"It's okay, Leanne," Uncle Tom said.

Brian, John, and Sam followed them. Uncle Tom hobbled slowly behind Madison and they came up to Mr. Merton who was just climbing down from the float.

"Sam, Brian," Madison said, "will you let me do something on my own with Dad?"

Brian stopped and nodded. Madison held out her hand to him and Brian put Mr. Merton's box in her hand.

"What's this all about? We'll be right back, buddy," Uncle Tom said to Brian and gave him a pat on the shoulder. Sam understood and turned around but she heard Madison talk.

"Mr. Merton," Madison said.

"Well, hello there," he said. His wrinkles swallowed up his eyes in a big grin. "Who's this you got with ya?"

"This is my dad who was wounded in Afghanistan," she said.

Sam walked back to the sidewalk with the boys but she watched the old man and Uncle Tom and Madison from where she was.

Uncle Tom and Mr. Merton shook hands and then Madison started talking. Her red bangs bounced as she shook her head and gestured with her hands. Sam saw Mr. Merton's face lose its smile as Madison talked. Then, she bent her head and Sam could see that she was shaking with sobs. Uncle Tom and Mr. Merton both frowned while they watched Madison. Then Madison threw her arms around Mr. Merton. Uncle Tom nodded and waited for Madison to release Mr. Merton. Madison pulled away, wiped tears from her eyes and handed the medal back to its owner.

Sam wasn't sure what happened next, but Mr. Merton's face regained its big smile. He turned to Uncle Tom and gave him another hearty handshake. Then he looked across the street to the rest of Sam's family and gave them a wave. He spoke to Uncle Tom as Madison clutched her dad's arm. One more round of handshakes and Madison and her dad made their way slowly back to join the family. The police stood by their cars.

"What was that all about?" Aunt Leanne asked.

Uncle Tom put his arm around Madison.

"Well, just a couple of dads talking about valor and doing the right thing," he mused. "And how things can get better when dads come home." He looked Madison in the eye and Sam could see they had an understanding. "Any chance we can get some ice cream?"

"It's that way," John pointed.

The family started walking, everyone trying to tell what happened over the weekend and then straining to hear Tom's story of how he got to Seattle and made the decision to come to Whidbey Island. Jenny pulled Madison aside and Sam saw her slip her the cell phone.

"Wow, ice cream for lunch!" Sam asked. "I'm sure going to remember this weekend."

From Sam's Top Secret Journal:

I told Jenny Madison wasn't bad. I know she did a bad thing but she learned something about herself, at least thats what Dad said. Dad always says that nobody is perfect, we just have to try hard every day to be better. Sometimes I don't know how to do better. I know, I should still try.

I learned what valor means this week. I also learned that sometimes we have to make mistakes to learn. I wonder if Kacey has someone in her life to help her with mistakes. I hope so.

Someday, if I am going to be on my own, I will make mistakes. That scares me.

20595300R00072

Made in the USA
San Bernardino, CA
16 April 2015